THE VISOKO CHRONICLE

OTHER TITLES IN THE SERIES

Prague Tales
Jan Neruda

Skylark
Dezső Kosztolányi

Be Faithful Unto Death
Zsigmond Móricz

The Doll
Bolesław Prus

The Adventures of Sindbad
Gyula Krúdy

The Sorrowful Eyes of Hannah Karajich
Ivan Olbracht

The Birch Grove and Other Stories
Jaroslaw Iwaszkiewicz

The Coming Spring
Stefan Żeromski

The Poet and the Idiot and Other Stories
Friedebert Tuglas

The Slave Girl and Other Stories on Women
Ivo Andrić

Martin Kačur—The Biography of an Idealist
Ivan Cankar

Whitehorn's Windmill or, The Unusual Events Once upon a Time in the Land of Paudruvė
Kazys Boruta

The Tower and Other Stories
Jānis Ezeriņš

A Tale of Two Worlds
Vjenceslav Novak

Three Chestnut Horses
Margita Figuli

Georgian Notes on the Caucasus—Three Stories
Aleksandre Qazbegi

The House of a Thousand Floors
Jan Weiss

Avala Is Falling
Biljana Jovanovic

THE VISOKO CHRONICLE

Ivan Tavčar

Translated by *Timothy Pogačar*

Central European University Press

Budapest–Vienna–New York

Published in 2021 by

Central European University Press

Nádor utca 9, H-1051 Budapest, Hungary
Tel: +36-1-327-3138 or 327-3000
E-mail: ceupress@press.ceu.edu
Website: www.ceupress.com

ISBN 978-963-386-433-3 (paperback)
ISBN 978-963-386-434-0 (ebook)
ISSN 1418-0162

Library of Congress Cataloging-in-Publication Data

Names: Tavčar, Ivan, 1851-1923, author. | Pogacar, Timothy, translator.
Title: The Visoko chronicle / Ivan Tavčar ; translated by Timothy
  Pogačar.
Other titles: Visoška kronika. English
Description: Budapest ; New York : Central European University Press, 2021.
  | Series: CEU press classics, 1418-0162 | Includes bibliographical
  references.
Identifiers: LCCN 2021045288 (print) | LCCN 2021045289 (ebook) | ISBN
  9789633864333 (paperback) | ISBN 9789633864340 (pdf)
Subjects: LCGFT: Novels.
Classification: LCC PG1918.T38 V513 2021 (print) | LCC PG1918.T38 (ebook)
  | DDC 891.8/435--dc23/eng/20211109
LC record available at https://lccn.loc.gov/2021045288
LC ebook record available at https://lccn.loc.gov/2021045289

Contents

Introduction to
The Visoko Chronicle

A small iron, black chest belonging to the Kalan family, the one-time owners of the Visoko estate, sits on the floor of a room in the Škofja Loka Museum, housed in the Škofja Loka castle. The room in which the chest rests contains eighteenth-century furnishings belonging to the Kalan family. A visitor encounters it by passing through a room displaying some of the Tavčar family's furniture. Ivan and his wife Franja acquired the estate near Ivan's birth village of Poljane in 1893, living there and in Ljubljana until the writer's death in 1923. The sequence of museum exhibits neatly ties the Kalan family, to which the novel's narrator Izidor belongs, to the author of the novel. The black chest is a key to understanding Ivan Tavčar's novel, *The Visoko Chronicle*. It signals the importance of ownership both of material things—first among them the Visoko estate—and of self.

In the novel, the Kalans' chest becomes the war chest that Izidor's father Polikarp brings home from mercenary service in the Thirty Years War. Polikarp purchases Visoko with the ill-gotten gold, which is also the source of Izidor's covetousness and the trauma he suffers at his father's hands in chapter 1. The chest, then, binds father and son by means of the estate that is passed on (conditionally) and by virtue of the inherited guilt and requisite repentance that come with it. The totality of what Izidor inherits also jeopardizes his individuality. While he prospers as owner of the estate through much of the novel and seemingly grows in public standing, the denouement—his intended bride Agata's trial for witchcraft—reveals his lack of freedom. His individuality remains subjugated to the social hierarchy and religious beliefs, and his father's original sin.

Close father-son relations are underlined by parallels in their lives: both are forced from home at age twelve; at age twenty-seven, both visit the area where Polikarp commits a murder when returning from the war; and both marry at age forty-three. The parallels are the narrator Izidor's (unwitting?) contrivance. The title page of his chronicle displays the year 1695, when Agata's trial for witchcraft takes place. The realizations he comes to afterwards could be the reason for patterning the account of his life on his father's life. His name also points to an important paternal connection: Isidore the Laborer (d. 636, feast day 15 May), patron of farmers, and Isidore of Chios (d. 251, feast day 14 May), military patron, unite father and son's occupations. Following the trial, Izidor joins the army and fights in the War of Spanish Succession (1701–14).[1] Incidentally, the reader may wish

---

[1] Miran Hladnik, "Tavčarjeva *Visoška kronika*," in *Esej na maturi 2006: V vrtincu zločina in krivde*, ed. Rajko Korošec (Ljubljana: Intelego, 2005), 73.

to check meanings associated with other main characters' names, in particular those of Izidor's brother Jurij (George) and eventual bride, Margareta (popularly Marjeta, Marjetica, Meta), one of the most popular names of virtuous female characters in Slovene literature.[2] The names of many other characters in the novel, from the bishop who presides over the trial to residents of the town of Škofja Loka, are historically attested, though their roles are fictional.

The novel's structure also highlights the father-son relationship. Chapters 1 to 3 are set at Visoko and in Škofja Loka, and 4 to 6 in the nearby German area called Davča and Visoko. In these chapters, Izidor recounts his boyhood and youth. Another set of three chapters, 8 to 10, focus on Visoko after Agata's arrival, and 11 to 13 are about her trial in Škofja Loka. Chapter 7, in which Polikarp dies, is set off against 14, wherein Izidor departs for the army. Further, the first six chapters end with the annulment of Izidor's first engagement, to his maternal cousin Margareta, and chapters 11 to 13 conclude with his loss of Agata. Polikarp intervenes in the first instance; Izidor's failings are responsible in the second.

The title of the novel and the first-person narration point to the fact that the work is, in one regard, a family chronicle set in the seventeenth century and with enough historical background and color to qualify it as a historical novel. Chief among the historical events pro-

[2] Miran Hladnik, *Slovenski zgodovinski roman* (Ljubljana: Filozofska fakulteta, 2009), 151–54.

viding a backdrop to the novel are the Thirty Years War (1618–48) and the Counter-Reformation. (Both have early twentieth-century analogies to which we will return.) The lands the Slovenes inhabited in the seventeenth century were not directly involved in the Thirty Years War; Polikarp Khallan was a mercenary in different armies. The narrator puts the war's cause down to Martin Luther and the Reformation, a gross oversimplification but one that conforms to his views. The war was, of course, not primarily a confessional conflict.[3] Political, economic, climatic, and other factors played roles over the decades in what came to be remembered—in particular in Germany—as Europe's greatest tragedy until the twentieth-century world wars. Tavčar was attuned to German Romantic views of the war as a cause of the country's slow development. The war is not of personal historical interest but one of its chief results, a long-lasting fascination with violence and death (an estimated eight million perished) on the continent,[4] is evident in his works, including *The Visoko Chronicle*. Yet Tavčar appears aware of this attraction and lampoons it in chapter 8, where a Škofja Loka burgher asks a local artist to depict the dismemberment of a traitor in the Austrian army.

The Counter-Reformation in central Slovene lands interested Tavčar. The motif of religious differences—between Roman Catholicism and Lutheranism—splitting families is prominent in his historical fiction;

---

[3] Peter H. Wilson, *The Thirty Years War: Europe's Tragedy* (Cambridge, MA: Harvard University Press, 2009), 9.

[4] Wilson, *The Thirty Years War*, 5.

for example, in the novella "Vita vitae meae" (1883), which, along with the novel *Grajski pisar* (The castle scribe, 1889), describes religious strife. Both are set during the Counter-Reformation in Carniola. Tavčar uses historical sources referring to his home region for these works, in particular August Dimitz's *Geschichte Krains von den ältesten Rücksicht auf Kulterentwicklung.*[5] The two works of historical fiction are set in 1585 and 1587, two years for which Dimitz had Škofja Loka archival materials.[6]

The *Visoko Chronicle* as well is set in the Poljanska Valley and the town of Škofja Loka. Polikarp is a secret Protestant, as is Agata's grandmother. Polikarp's faith repels his wife and son Izidor. Lutheranism persisted longer in this region,[7] making Polikarp's adherence plausible. The earlier works portray both Catholics and Protestants as intolerant, even to their own family members.[8] Leaving aside Izidor's blind faith in the Catholic Church, which represents social conformism more than religious belief, *The Visoko Chronicle* provides a more tempered view of organized religion than previous works. For instance, the

---

[5] August Dimitz, *Geschichte Krains von den ältesten Rücksicht auf Kulterentwicklung* (Laibach: Kleinmayr & Bamberg, 1874).

[6] Pavle Blaznik, "Reformacija in protireformacija na tleh loškega gospostva," *Loški razgledi* 9 (1966): 71–104.

[7] Akenka Jensterle Doležal, "Reprezentacija protestantov ('luterancev') v zgodovinskih tekstih Ivana Tavčarja: Med zgodovino, fikcijo in ideologijo," *Slavia centralis* 12.1 (2019): 325–26; Pavle Blaznik, "Reformacija in protireformacija na tleh loškega gospostva," *Loški razgledi* 9 (1966): 71–104.

[8] Akenka Jensterle Doležal, "Reprezentacija protestantov ('luterancev') v zgodovinskih tekstih Ivana Tavčarja: Med zgodovino, fikcijo in ideologijo," *Slavia centralis* 12.1 (2019): 328.

Catholic bishop is the one who brings sanity to the witch-craft proceedings, and Izidor complies with his dying father's request for a visit by a Protestant minister.

It is tempting to associate Polikarp's non-conformism and rugged individualism with Protestantism, but Tavčar's interest in the philosophic aspects of the Reformation is dubious, even though, like other young Slovene radicals of the 1870s,[9] he was enamored of Henry Buckle's *History of Civilization in England*, which championed Protestantism (he read it in German). His liberal convictions might also be reason to assume an interest in Protestant thinking, but Slovene liberalism, while it acknowledged European liberal philosophy and affirmed basic maxims (e.g., individual liberty), tended to devalue liberal beliefs for political expediency.[10] The liberal party was essentially an anti-clerical (anti-Catholic) organization.

After Dimitz, historiography on Protestantism in Slovene lands coincides chronologically with Tavčar's earlier historical fiction. The first studies date to the 1880s;[11] France Kidrič's authoritative book on the father of the Slovene Reformation, Primož Trubar (1508–86), appeared in 1908, the year the foundation for a monument to Trubar was placed in Ljubljana's Tivoli Park. At the time, a contributor to the leading liberal journal, *Ljubljanski zvon*, asserted that the Reformation and previous peas-

---

[9] Marja Boršnik, *Fran Celestin* (Ljubljana: DZS, 1951), 70–71.

[10] Jurij Perovšek, *Liberalizem in vprašanje slovenstva: Nacionalna politika liberalnega tabora v letih 1918–1929* (Ljubljana: Modrijan, 1996) 14–15.

[11] For example, in Josip Stare, *Obća zgodovina za slovensko ljudstvo* (Celovec: Družba sv. Mohorja, 1874–88); Ivan Križanič, *Zgodovina svete katoliške cerkve* (Celovec: Družba sv. Mohorja, 1883–87).

ant rebellions had the same root cause, the desire for greater freedom.[12] Tavčar spoke at the laying of the foundation. After chastising Catholic opposition to it, he expressed admiration for Trubar's linguistic work—writing a catechism and prayers in Slovene—but did not draw liberal conclusions that might have been expected. A possible explanation for Tavčar's reluctance was probably the social alignment of Protestantism with German culture at a time when Slovene nationalists opposed German influence in the Slovene provinces of the empire. Indeed, animosity to Germans is evident in *The Visoko Chronicle.*

On the other hand, Tavčar's emphasis on Trubar's linguistic achievement—he had laid the groundwork for the first Slovene grammar, *Arcticae horulae* (1584) by Adam Bohorič—was in line with the Slovene nineteenth-century nation building project, in which language rights were central. A popular view today is that Trubar's had a "mission toward independent thinking, national identity, and education," and that "the people of Slovenia are still grateful for the accomplishments... which gave them the basis for their language and national identity."[13] It is more accurate to see Trubar—and Tavčar surely did—as having posited the principle that language and ethnic group, not yet nation, are associated in a space.[14]

---

[12] Ivan Merhar, "Primož Trubar," *Ljubljanski zvon* (1908): 514–25.

[13] "2008: The Year of Primož Trubar," *Prosveta* (Pittsburgh), 27 August 2008.

[14] Jože Pogačnik, "The Cultural Significance of the Protestant Reformation in the Genesis of the South Slav Nations," *Slovene Studies* 6.1–2 (1984): 109.

The Reformation and Counter-Reformation, which pitted Slovene speakers and different classes against one another (imperial and ecclesiastic vs. lower nobility and towns) had an analogy in Tavčar's time with political divisions and town vs. countryside. Tavčar saw societal divisions, as well as emigration, as threats to the nation that would not attain statehood until the late twentieth century.[15] The obvious parallel of the Thirty Years War was World War One, which was a calamity for the Slovene people.[16] Over 29,000 soldiers' deaths have been documented,[17] and estimates run to 40,000, or three percent of the population;[18] a substantial amount of territory inhabited by Slovenes was lost to Austria and Italy. The greater historical background alludes to internal and external threats to the nation in the early twentieth century.

The Visoko Chronicle is local history as well. The villages, churches, and geographic locations that figure in the novel—not to mention the places in the town of

---

[15] Miran Hladnik compares the Catholic-Protestant opposition in the novel to the Christian-pagan contest in France Prešeren's "Krst pri Savici ("The Baptism on the Savica"), rivalries between Catholic conservatives vs. liberals, and the conflict between the Home Guards and the Partisans during World War Two (*Slovenski zgodovinski roman*, 229)—all of which sharply divided Slovene society.

[16] A 2008–2009 exhibit organized by the Institute for Contemporary History in Ljubljana, *Slovenci in prva svetovna vojna, 1914–1918* (Slovenes and the First World War, 1914–1918) illustrated the war's tremendous impact. See: https://www.sistory.si/11686/1160.

[17] https://zv1.sistory.si/?lang=sl.

[18] The population of today's Slovene territory in the 1910 Austrian census was 1,320,000. Zdenko Čepič et al., *Zgodovina Slovencev* (Ljubljana: Cankarjeva založba, 1979), 540.

Škofja Loka—can be visited today. Tavčar was born in Poljane and baptized at St. Martin's church, a short distance from his birth house (a commemorative bust stands by the house), just as Izidor was in 1664. (The Yugoslav government had the church destroyed in 1954.) One can follow the way Izidor walked from Visoko and the village of Poljane, around Mt. Blegoš, to the Davča Valley to propose to Margareta, and make it in a day, as he did. The central site of historical interest is, of course, the Visoko manor. A one-room museum devoted to the writer is now located on the first floor of the partially restored house that dates to the mid-eighteenth century. Tavčar's purchase of the estate in 1893 and semi-permanent return—return to the village is a recurring motif in his works—motivated the writing of the novel.

A visitor to Škofja Loka's well preserved center can see places Izidor mentions in the novel—for example, town gates, the granary, and castle. The castle is probably the most well known in Slovenia. Rebuilt in 1513–16 after an earthquake in 1511, it houses the Škofja Loka museum. The jailer shows young Izidor the dungeons, which terrify him.[19] Below the town wall, the confluence of two branches of the Sora River is the site of Agata's trial. Izidor's visits to Škofja Loka highlight the town-countryside (urban-rural) divide that, transposed onto Tavčar's time, vexed Slovene liberals. The writer was, of course, acutely aware of it, given his rural roots.

---

[19] The treatment of prisoners was in fact worse than recounted in the novel. See: Ivan Stopar, *Gradovi na Slovenskem* (Ljubljana: Cankarjeva založba, 1986), 233.

The Visoko Chronicle is a historical novel with a pan-European backdrop and strong local focus, but it also has attributes of a domestic novel, a Bildungsroman, an anti-war novel, and a rural novel.[20] At least one critic casts it as a psychological novel centering on the father-son relationship.[21] Readers naturally have varying opinions on genre and meaning. Some may even consider it a work for younger readers. It is true that the novel is required reading in the second year of Slovene high school—but then so is *War and Peace*. And *The Visoko Chronicle* presents some challenges to secondary school readers.[22] Certainly some will find the descriptions of rural life charming and be drawn to the topic of witchcraft.

Church and secular authorities handling of witchcraft allegations changed through the Middle Ages and early modern period. During the time we are concerned with, there was an increase in accusations in the late sixteenth century because of environmental and social problems. The increase continued until the ravages of the Thirty Years War drained enthusiasm for witch hunts.[23]

---

[20] Miran Hladnik, *Slovenski zgodovinski roman*, 148. A rural novel (*kmečki roman*) is a genre popular in Slovenia from the mid-nineteenth to the mid-twentieth century. It typically revolves around possession of a farm and related family tensions. See: Miran Hladnik, *Slovenska kmečka povest* (Ljubljana: Prešernova družba, 1990).

[21] Marijan Kramberger, "Kako brati Visoško kroniko," in Ivan Tavčar, *Visoška kronika* (Maribor: Obzorja, 1968), 188–201.

[22] Jožica Jožef Beg, "The Historical Novel as a Basis for Developing Linguistic and Literary Competence in Secondary School Literature Classes," *Slovene Studies* 42.2 (2000): 149–68

[23] Wilson, *The Thirty Years War*, 842–43.

Tavčar's description of Agata's trial and the townsfolk's reactions, especially the women's, are entertaining, but it contains two historical anomalies. First, torture was typically employed to extract the names of co-conspirators,[24] but in the novel it is proposed out of wanton lust. Second, the bishop handling the proceedings and trial by water advises Izidor (chapter 11) that should Agata emerge from the river alive, her innocence will be proven. This is in fact the opposite of how a water trial went: If a person floated—that is, if the water (analogous to baptismal water) rejected the body—then she or he was guilty. Unfortunately, proof of innocence meant death.[25] None of this detracts from Tavčar's fictionalized portrayal of the event.

Regarding Tavčar's biography: He was born and grew up in Poljane, about twelve kilometers from Škofja Loka. The peasant family with eight children was poor, subsisting on three hectares of land. At age nine, Tavčar was enrolled in the St. Aloysius primary school in Ljubljana, but had to transfer to a Franciscan-run school in Novo Mesto after a curfew violation—a nighttime visit to a suburban mansion owned by an industrialist whose daughter he adored. The writer's nationalist opinions took shape in Novo Mesto. He finished gymnasium in Ljubljana (1868–71), then one-year military service, writ-

---

[24] Wilson, *The Thirty Years War*, 842.

[25] Péter Tóth G., "River Ordeal—Trial by Water—Swimming of Witches: Procedures of Ordeal in Witch Trials," in *Witchcraft Mythologies and Persecutions*, eds. Gábor Klaniczay and Éva Pócs, Series Demons, Spirits, Witches, vol. 3 (Budapest–New York: Central European University Press, 2008), 136–37.

ing, and scholarships supported him during law school in Vienna (1871–74). Vienna's intellectual opportunities did not outweigh dismay at his austere living conditions and yearning for home. Life was even more difficult because his parents did not support his choice of study, preferring he enter the priesthood. But it was in Vienna that he became acquainted with world literature and began to write more. His early stories link female characters with life's tragedies.[26] Other stories link love, weakness, and death. An early sketch, "Margareta," points to later developments in Tavčar's prose: the narrator has lost touch with nature and love after years of city life but rediscovers them through a childhood friend who, of course, dies in his arms when he visits his home near Škofja Loka.

After law school, he was apprenticed to an attorney in Ljubljana for two years, where he was active in a nationalist club, a literary club, and a drama society. From 1877 to 1880 he worked in a law office in Kranj, then in another office in Ljubljana before opening his own practice in 1883. The passivity of many of Tavčar's characters contrasts with his robust public demeanor. He was an engaging speaker and forceful author of feuilletons for the newspaper *Slovenski narod*. In the 1880s, he become active in literary journalism, serving as editor of the liberal journal *Ljubljanski zvon* (1881–84). He parted with the journal because he considered the other editors too moderate. The 1880s saw the publication of argua-

---

[26] France Bernik, "Erotika v nekaterih Tavčarjevih proznih delih," *Slavistična revija* 22 (1972): 42.

bly his best works, a collection of sketches set in his home region entitled *Med gorami* (In the mountains, 1876–88). He published a historical novel entitled *Janez Solnce* in the journal *Slovan*, which he founded with his political ally Ivan Hribar in 1884. (The novel attracted more attention because of its allusions to contemporary politics than for its historical content.)

At age thirty-five, in May 1887, Tavčar married Franica Košenini, from a wealthy Ljubljana family. The couple purchased a large, two-story house in the town center on the Ljubljanica river. He began quickly climbing the social ladder. For example, he was elected chairman of the national publishing house in 1888. Throughout the 1880s, he jousted with the Catholic clergy, who he thought ought not be involved in politics. But the Catholic People's Party's following increased in the 1890s as that of the liberals' declined. While Tavčar's national influence waned, he continued to serve in the provincial (Carniolan) parliament (–1912), was a representative in Vienna (1901–1906), and was elected mayor of Ljubljana (1911–21). He did not hold elected office after that but was director of food supplies after the war and was briefly involved in constitutional negotiations in the Yugoslav capital of Belgrade in 1920. Though he previously considered Slovenia's prospects would be better within a post-war Austria, he was enthusiastic about the new Yugoslav state. When he died in Ljubljana in February 1923, a large cortege accompanied his coffin drawn by horses to the Ljubljana train station for the trip to Škofja Loka and then on to Visoko, where he was buried.

Tavčar's last two major works, the novella *Cvetje v je-seni* (*Autumn Blossoms*, 1917)[27] and *The Visoko Chronicle*, serialized in the journal *Ljubljanski zvon* throughout 1919, are both set in the Poljanska Valley and feature the motif of return and the theme of love, which in all its forms is the most important theme in Tavčar's writings. Love of his homeland, the Poljanska Valley and Slovenia, lie at the heart of *The Visoko Chronicle*. On the Visoko grounds there is a large bronze statue of the writer in a powerful pose, gazing towards the village of Poljane,[28] back in time to his home to which he returned, just as Izidor finally did.

---

[27] The English title is taken from Savo Tory's self-published (no place or date) translation.

[28] I argue in a forthcoming article in the *Slavic and East European Journal* that Tavčar may just as well be looking westward in general, given that the statue was made possible by a distant relative from Poljane who emigrated to the US, John Thatcher. The statue was placed in 1957.

THE VISOKO CHRONICLE

EMIL LEON BOWS TO MY WIFE FRANČIŠKA,
THE PRESENT LADY OF VISOKO

I.

I was born in the year of Our Lord 1664, on the 1664
feast of St. Izidor, in this very place—Visoko. My
father was Polikarp Khallan, also Khallain, the
owner of two holdings at Visoko, and my mother was
Barbara Khallanin, also Khallainin, born at Suha, the
second daughter of the local farmer Volk Wulffing.

Father Karel Ignacij Codelli, then pastor at Poljane,
baptized me in honor of St. Izidor in the small church
of St. Martin. The baptism was talked about all over the
valley. I had eight godparents, four male and four female.
Such a quantity of Črni Kal wine was consumed at the
baptismal feast that Godfather Kožuh from Mount St.
Sobota and Godfather Hmeljinec from Mount St. Volnik quarreled and almost came to bloody blows. Because
of that, even then, farsighted women would say that the
child just born and baptized into the Christian faith
would encounter misfortune in this world. That talk—
may the Mother of God have mercy—later came to full
fruition, as anyone may conclude from these writings of
mine, which I resolved upon when I was like a winter
tree, without leaf or sap.

I only thank God that he endowed me with strength enough that my pen did not drop until it was written how I sinned, how I called God's wrath upon myself, and how I did too little penance for myself and for my father, Polikarp Khallan, who lived neither justly nor pleasingly to God. Even my childhood years were miserable, and I felt the weight of life pressing upon me like a burden, painful and bitter.

Who was my father Polikarp? Where did he come from? Where had he been before? God knows!

At the time I as yet knew nothing about all of this, I only sensed that Polikarp Khallan was a hard, dark, and heartless master into whose soul the sun never shone. He mistreated his lawful wife, who bore him my brother by five years younger, Jurij, and me, beyond all bounds. Our house was not a house blessed by God. We had more than others, we possessed enough of everything, but beneath no roof was there less prayer and such a plenitude of cursing as beneath ours. Our master knew the curses of the whole world. He cursed in the language spoken by the common folk in our parts, but he also called upon the devil in languages people speak in other lands. When later I traveled among foreigners, I realized that he cursed in German, in Italian, and even in Spanish. Thus, when he died he carried with him dossiers of such bloody sins that even today I pray that Polikarp Khallan's sins may be overlooked in heaven; otherwise I do not know how he will fare before his Judge in the other world.

When I began to come of age, my father was already fifty years old. And he was tall, like an apple tree, and sturdy, like the bear that rips sheep apart on Mount Blegoš. He spoke few words and no kind ones, and he stalked the hired lads and maids lest they loaf and shirk their work. Whomever he surprised was mercilessly beaten, often to within an inch of their lives.

God is my witness that my mother Barbara was the best housewife, who increased her master's wealth by all manner of frugality, while he would often shamelessly strike her gaunt face before the children and laborers, so that red blood flowed down her cheeks and over her bony chin. Only the Mother of God, who counted the tears of my humble mother, given a harsh fate, knows how often the tormented woman cried at night. And Visoko's savage and fretted master received no mercy; he cried out beneath the heavy burden with which he had saddled himself and he, too, groaned and sobbed at night, as if buried alive deep in the black earth.

After we received Jurij, my father no longer slept with his lawful partner. My brother and I and our mother passed our nights in the upper quarters. Father chose to spend his in the cellar. Even by day only a little light came into the cellar through two low, barred windows; dampness exuded from the plaster and crept down the black walls in large drops. Here, not long after Jurij's birth, he built himself a crude lair, which he made up himself and into which neither his wife nor the maidservants were permitted.

As I grew older and the light of the moon at times called me from my bed, I would steal up to the cellar and I hear how my father called out in his sleep, how he drove someone from his bed, how he howled and rasped. Night brought him no rest; it was as if someone were rolling a stone over him, causing the old man to despair beneath it, as if he had slipped under a mill wheel that crushed and pinned him deep in the water, preventing him from moving his limbs or releasing his pent-up breath.

I was twelve years old. It was then that my mother took me to town for the first time.

A man was trading in weapons right by the Poljane Gate. He was selling swords, heavy muskets, and iron helmets. Everything was rather old and used, since it had been left over from the war that had raged over the whole world because of a false faith—everywhere people had been murdered and their dwellings burned. The war left vast cemeteries and whole stockpiles of arms. Discharged soldiers as well as traders brought some of those arms to our bishop's town, Škofja Loka.

In those days I had a burning desire to become a soldier, and I was inspired when I saw the Loka trader's flintlock with a thick stock bound in bright metal. But it was so big that I, a boy, could hardly have carried it. The pistol instantly gripped my soul, and my heart yearned for it. "Buy it for me," I sighed to mother. She placed a hand on my shoulder and answered, "How can I buy it for you? I would have to pay a Venetian ducat for it!"

Soon after that the worst moment of my desolate life struck, one that later tormented me in broad daylight and roused me from a sleep filled with wild dreams.

In the afternoon, mother and I returned from Loka. Already at the footbridge below our Visoko home we heard my angry father's screaming. He was in the field, where the maidservants had failed to do something as it pleased him. In great fear we stole around the barn and into the house. There, mother hurried upstairs to quickly hide in her room, as she always did during such outbursts.

But I stopped right before the cellar and noticed at once that the door was ajar. When father had angrily stormed off to the field he forgot to lock the cellar door, which had not happened before or ever after. Like a wren, I shot into the gloomy space, surely drawn by Satan himself against the will of my timid soul!

At first, the gloominess struck me and my weakened sight could not distinguish one thing from another. But I got used to the place and when I did, I noticed a black iron chest on the carelessly made bed. It was shut, and try as I might, my little hand could not even budge it. Sweat covered my face and body and I was ready to run because it seemed that something horrible was stalking me in the dark corner. At that moment a ray of sunlight stole up from somewhere—God our judge sent it to strike the sinner in his own child—and shone in through the grate on the window, creating a bright stripe on the dark clay earth at my feet. Something golden lay on the stripe. Jesus and Mary! I bent over and a ducat lay in my hand, a gold Venetian ducat! And again I was standing before the trader in Loka and looking at the pistol with bright inlay that at that moment was first of all my youthful desires.

While I thought deeply about how I would buy myself the proud weapon, an iron fist seized the hand in which I squeezed the Venetian money. It was as if I had been snared. My father squeezed my hand so hard I could feel the ducat piercing the skin and flesh of my palm. He had returned to the cellar, but in my rapture I had not noticed his approach. He clasped my hand with his right hand and with his left grabbed some rags from the bed and threw them over the chest. My hand quivered, but so did my father's fist, because a terrible anger was ravaging him.

"Diavolo," he yelled, "you creep about the bed of your father, who gives you food and drink!" He dragged me along with him, not releasing my hand for an instant. Outside he pulled out his key with difficulty and, with even greater difficulty, locked the door to the cellar.

"You meant to steal!" The blood flowed to his face and his eyes flashed. I began to cry in terror, which only enraged my elder the more. He pulled me up the stairs and into the hallway, from the hallway into the room, and to the table, from which rose clouds of flies. The sun illuminated the whole room, setting the white wall and the ceiling above it aglow. In that glow my quivering soul caught sight of the crucifix in the corner and, on it, the white likeness of the Savior, bloodied and with a crown of thorns. "Christ help me," I groaned and tried to wrench my hand from my father's fist. "The devil help you," he roared and pressed my hand to the table so that my tiny fingers opened and the ducat flew from them, as a kernel flies from an ear of corn when grain is threshed on the floor.

"He stole, he stole from his own father!" In a haze I saw that his mouth was foaming. And I sobbed, "Father, I won't do it again!"

"You won't," he yelled hoarsely, "I'll make sure you won't!"

He uttered some curse in a foreign tongue. With his left hand he squeezed four of my fingers together so that only my little finger lay on the table. And then it happened!

"So you remember when it was that you stole!" With those words he grabbed the sharp Friulian hatchet that someone had left on the table. He swung it and cut off half my little finger, and the blood splattered on the table in thick droplets, as if a red rain were falling on it. My head whirled; the table, the ceiling, and Christ in the corner spun about me.

When I regained consciousness. I was writhing on the bench, pressing the poor mangled hand between my legs; my shirt, shoes, and the stockings above them— everything was bloody!

The family had gathered in the room. Mother was leaning against the stove, swooning again and again. She had been plaiting her hair when she heard my crying and my father's yells. Her hair still loose, she had hurried downstairs and now lay fainting by the stove. How gray her hair was already, and how sunken her face!

Mica the maid kept wetting her apron in a pot and wiping mother's forehead and cheeks with it, trying to bring her around. The little maid and the ox driver were praying out loud. Tonček, the herdsman, wailed as if someone were beating him with a birch rod.

Father remained standing at the table, clutching the hatchet in his right hand. The servant Lukež, who people said had been in the German wars with my father, stood fearlessly before him. They eyed each other like two vipers. Both were large-limbed and had the strength of beasts harnessed to the plow!

"Polikarp," Lukež commanded sharply, "put it down! May God forgive our sins: we slew children in Swabia and Saxony—you won't kill any more here! Especially not those born of your own flesh!"

The family began yelling, my brother Jurij lay on the floor and rolled around, crying and moaning.

"Put it down," Lukež kept repeating, "or I'll force you to, be you ten times my master! Who helped you when the Swedish cuirassier would have split your head? Who shot him through the neck so you could live? Think of that, Polikarp, and be a man, not a beast!"

At this argument father threw the hatchet under the bench, pressed both hands to his head, and running out of the room, screamed so terribly and horribly that I do not know whether ever afterwards I heard such a scream.

Yet once I did! I am certain! It was near Luzzara. Lord Eugenius was leading us and we were pounding the French. A young cornet pranced before our ranks, pointing at the enemy with his halberd. But in an instant, he fell and rolled in the dust! That time I heard exactly the same scream, because grapeshot from a cannon had shattered and ripped off both the cornet's legs!

1676 This happened to me in the 1676th year after the birth of our Lord and Savior.

My mother Barbara quietly and secretly buried the piece of my severed finger in the cemetery at St. Martin's church in Poljane. However, none of this remained a secret. The family was silent, but something of it none-theless slowly emerged and talk spread that there was someone at Visoko who was buried and yet was still walking about alive.

I was ill for a long time. The frail body of a twelve-year-old child could not endure such inhuman and rough treatment. Weakness overcame me and a terrible pain tortured me for several weeks. Prayer saved me—the whole house prayed for me—and the salve that Lukež brought from the German wars surely helped some, too. He sold it to others for a pretty penny, but charitably sacrificed a small wad to mother because he pitied me for having suffered such a cruel wound.

Mother applied the salve to my armpits for two nights in a row when I was delirious from the fever and pain. The treatment surely benefited me because the salve was concocted primarily from human fat—which was easy to come by in the German wars—boiled to-gether with white hair from the tail of a young cat that was black all over.

God has his ways when He wants to cure a sinner. Although many years have passed since they made peace in Germany—thus ending the war that had raged for thirty years in lands distant from us and which Martin Luther seduced into a false faith—we live in times that are accursed and evil and in all manner terrible. In such times the Lord Jesus must use all possible means—even human fat—if we are to be helped!

As I have written, I lay ill and in pain for a long time. The awareness of my body was impaired, and I lay as if in a sleep woven of bad dreams.

One day, I regained my senses. I was in the upper room, lying pleasantly on my mother's bed. I did not feel any pain or discomfort in my body.

My right hand lay on the covers, wrapped in a thick bandage, looking like a horse's hoof. The bandaged hand reminded me of what had happened, and I felt so woebegone that I began to sob quietly.

Suddenly a soft hand rested on my forehead and someone asked, "Do you recognize me? Do you know who I am? Poor suffering soul of mine!"

How could I not know that beloved face when on Judgment Day I will recognize it among the countless multitudes, even from a distance! "Mother!" I cried joyfully and tried to raise my bandaged hand to embrace her. But I could not lift the hand, as terrible pain shot through it.

She asked, "What would you like to eat?" I did not want to eat, but she lamented that I was eating almost nothing.

With great tenderness she drew my good hand out of the covers, and indeed the fingers on it were nothing but thin bones!

She wanted to go and warm some milk up for me. She also told me that she would crumble in some white bread, which we only had in the house on the most significant holidays.

But I would not be consoled; I began to cry and, in agony, cried out, "Have father come!"

With that something was revealed to the poor woman that she had never suspected. The blood rushed to her heart and she was as white as a corpse. Angrily she refused me:

"Quiet, my dear, and do not speak of that, that …"

She chased after the right word but could not seize it. She meant to say something else but changed her mind and then simply sighed, "…of that Lutheran!"

Noticing I was stunned, she sobbed:

"I told you noth-, nothing…!" She left the room downhearted. And my feverish head began to work like the gears inside a clock.

My father, a Lutheran! He would never enter heaven! His faith was not my faith! If it leaks out, everyone will despise him! The magistrate of the Loka castle will send for him and they will condemn him to death! Then they will cut off his head! And for me that head was the most beautiful in the whole world! Oh Jesus! Oh Jesus! Oh Jesus!

I trembled before him, but when he moved logs that two men could not move, or broke a horse that threw everyone else from the saddle, I was happy that I had such a father!

And father did come! One afternoon, when mother was milking in the barn, he came to me. It was apparent that he had gone even grayer; contrary to his custom he had let his beard grow, and it was pure white.

He hesitated for a moment at the door; with his large build, he almost reached the ceiling. Step by step he came closer to me.

I was losing consciousness and I contemplated him the way a dove contemplates a hawk.

He moved the chair towards my bed and, on the covers before me, placed a leather gauntlet, partially covered with iron, of the kind the Swedish cavalry once wore. He sat right in front of me and in a hollow voice called to me:

"Izidor, throw it in my face!" I did not move, at which he loudly yelled, "Throw it!" Strange lines formed around his mouth and a deep crease cut across his forehead, which meant that he was becoming angry.

I fearfully took the gauntlet and hurled it at my father's face, which he was craning towards me.

And the iron must have struck the old man hard, since blood appeared on his face. Polikarp groaned:

"It is right that my own child punishes me with such disdain!"

He reached for my small hand and bent his iron-like head over it. He uttered not a word; only his body trembled from time to time as he shook with remorse.

Tears welled up in my eyes and I sobbed: "Father, I'm not upset anymore."

He hurried away from me. As he crossed the room his legs became entangled, as if he had drunk too much wine. I well know that Polikarp Khallan seldom drank to excess and that he was sober that afternoon, too.

My left hand was wet, wet from the tears my proud father had shed!

He never spoke to me about what happened. But several days later, when I awoke in the morning, a pistol with a thick, metal-bound stock lay on my covers.

So began the days of my penance, which I did for my whole life for my own trespasses and also for the trespasses of my father, who was my most severe and unsparing master. I had to give up everything that makes a man happy, and still I continue to beg God Our Creator to be pleased with my penance and, in eternal life, not to separate me from the one who fathered me.

II.

_____

A t last I recovered.

Immediately after that my father, who probably did not like the sight of my crippled hand, gave me to Ahac Langerholz in Škofja Loka. The latter had a smithy outside the city walls, near where the waters of the Selščica and Poljanščica Rivers meet. For three years I worked there, because Polikarp Khallan wanted to have his own private blacksmith at Visoko.

I went to live at Kašper Wohlgemuet's, who, after the last great fire, had built himself a beautiful new house on the square. There he kept his famous beer hall.

For three years I lived among strangers. I also grew accustomed to the language spoken by the people who have come and settled among us from German lands.

During those three years I never went to Visoko. I was not even summoned when my mother died. They buried her without me. However, the moment that she died was revealed to me. On the night she left this world there was such an explosion in the Wohlgemuet house, where I was sleeping, that at first I thought they had fired the cannon at the castle. It told me that Barbara Khallan had gone out like a lamp whose oil has run dry.

She had no difficulties before her Judge, because her life was a bed of thorns; those thorns stabbed her, even though she had no wish but to serve God in his true faith!

During the years I was learning to be a smith, I experienced nothing special. At first, I was wide-eyed because I was not used to the large town. But Master Langerholz took care that I did not wander about and chase the curiosities of beautiful Škofja Loka. He taught me by word, but also with his fist, and I might record that I received many more blows from him than kind words. Nor did my relative Wohlgemuet overfill my bowl. Therefore, I often cried late into the night in the attic, where it was either stifling or freezing, so that sleep would not close my eyes.

I also experienced pleasant days. Especially pleasant were the fairs on the square, which attracted many people, among them the corrupt, so that the then esteemed and respected town judge, Janez Kos, had difficulties with them.

The most amusing thing for me, and the most bother for the town judge, was provided by the students of the Jesuit fathers in Ljubljana. They came to town on different occasions, whether they had school or not. It was said that these students seldom went to school and provided their father prefect with some very tortured days.

When the news burst forth that the students were singing in the town square, we apprentices disappeared from the smithy, causing the master to rage and later to pay us back in the most bitter coin. Nothing could stop us! Each time we hurried to the square and listened to the singing. We gave the students nothing because we had nothing ourselves, but the burghers and country men and women had to take up a collection for them. Yet these students did not live poorly; if they weren't paid, other people's possessions would even disappear in their hands.

One holiday afternoon they performed a touching *actio* for us, and we were all so pleased that we even cried. And at every opportunity they knew how to work it so there would be dancing. Then they would take the girls from the local youths, which led to anger and fights.

They even fought with the butchers' helpers and showed not the least deference to the town guards. It was no wonder they finally angered the lord mayor of the town and he forbade them entry. What a shame! The adults and we youngsters bitterly complained about that prohibition!

We boys were not allowed to enter the castle. Yet the huge edifice with its immense tower excited my curiosity most of all. I was told how many heavy cannons were stationed behind the wall and how elegantly his lord the castle magistrate lived inside. There were also unbelievable stories about the chambers where the lord bishop himself stayed when he came to Loka and was met by the town elders at the Water Gate.

Unfortunately, there was no such visit while I was apprenticed to Langerholz. But I did often go to the high vaulted bridge, which, it is said and written, has no rival in all of Germany. When swimming, the Loka boys jumped from the bridge into the water, but no one was ever known to have been hurt doing so. They tried to convince me to jump but couldn't since it was indeed too high.

Yet I did get into the castle! The jailer, Mihol Schwaiffstrigkh, had ordered a new hammer from our master. One morning I brought it to him. My heart beat as, inside the town wall, I made my way upwards and came to the dark castle entrance, which opened before me like a black maw. Fearfully I crept into the spacious courtyard, where the jailer Mihol, sitting on a small chair, sleepily worked his thread. He was at work, but when he had a bit of free time he mended shoes and so earned a part of his daily bread with his thread. Despite his merciless calling, he was always in good humor and people in Loka society were happy to see him, even though he was close to the executioner, whom it was shameful to touch and whose company it was a misfortune to keep!

He took the hammer and asked me to whom I belonged and where I was from. I told him that I was from Visoko. He exclaimed merrily:

"Then you're Polikarp's! Why the hell doesn't he come to Loka anymore to make his payments, he hasn't spent anything for a drink for a long time?!"

He stood up and put aside his apron. "Boy," he said, "you've stopped by on the right day. The lord magistrate is in Ljubljana. If he were here, the old devil wouldn't allow cobbling in the courtyard! He's at a meeting of the estates, where he can indulge in any pleasure he desires, as far as I care."

He noticed that I was running my eyes over the tall tower and the buildings that huddled around it like chicks. He freely offered:

"Would you like to look around a little? Fine, fine! You're getting to the age when you will be plagued by sin from all sides; so, it won't hurt if today I show you what good medicine we have in the Loka castle against all types of transgressions. We cure murder, manslaughter, thievery, and everything else you shouldn't know about just yet."

He went for his lamp and a heavy key. Then he led me to some stairs that ran beside the tower and deep beneath the earth. There, he opened an iron gate and we arrived in a cellar into which the sun did not shine by day or the stars at night. He lit the lamp, but even with the light I had difficulty moving my trembling legs. Drops fell from the plaster and a cold draft blew from I knew not where.

"The worst of the worst sinners come here!" With these words the jailer raised a wooden cover. "There," he continued and pointed out some sort of well, "we lower criminals who are condemned to death. God protect you, child, that you never fall into my hands! We lower them into this pit on a rope, and then they are graciously allowed to make a nice nest, as it pleases them, in this beautiful dwelling. We're always fair judges! They can neither lie down nor sit, but they have full liberty to stand, first on one foot and then on the other. Usually some water gathers below, and they stand in it, which is good if it forces the blood to a man's head. We wash them for a while, then hand them over to the law clean, and then choke them on Gavžnik. Yes, boy, we work precisely and conscientiously!"

He showed me yet other lockups, the most narrow, dark holes, into which they cast prisoners like piglets into a pen. When he shone the light inside, rats and mice ran into cracks in the walls. You could not lie or stand in those lockups. Each was so short that you couldn't stretch out your legs, and could sleep only bent double, if you were able to fall asleep at all with your head on the cold, hard stone!

"Now I'll show you a special little room," Mihol boasted, and opened the door to the last lockup.

It was an empty, high-ceilinged room that looked just as if it were cut out of a cliff. Two large iron cuffs were stuck in the ceiling and one more in the stone floor.

"Here," explained Schwaiffstrigkh, "is where they bring criminals when the lord magistrate questions them under torture." He quickly added, "But that's not my duty. The executioner, who is usually called from Ljubljana and whom I have yet to lay eyes on, does all of that. I wouldn't want to watch the questioning, even if I were allowed to, because I don't like watching a man sitting on the Spanish horse, or having his fingers or feet crushed in a press, or hanging in these shackles. Believe me, lad, if you're hanging in shackles from the ceiling and being pulled by the legs with a rope through the lower shackle, and your limbs begin to crack and groan, it's not a portion of paradise! So you see, we have the very best things, just too many of them. A man has to have a strong stomach to endure it all!"

After that he continued: "The last person to hang in the shackles was Lucija Muhliceva from Bukovščica. That was under my predecessor, because at the time I was still learning to mend shoes. She caused dysentery among the people and had a pact with the devil. She certainly wailed terribly when they stretched her between the shackles in here. In the end they hanged her and while she hung they burned her on a pyre. Therefore, we are merciful judges, for we could have burned her alive."

We were passing by a little door. "Here is the room where the weapons that are needed when we question sinners under torture are kept. The executioner has the key. Most of the goods are the property of the high estates; they kindly help us when we're in need of something."

I was covered with sweat when we stepped back into the courtyard. And what I had been shown bore so deeply into my soul that I was about to be sick. And ever after, when the devil pursued me with the temptation to take another's belongings or even another's life, my memory returned me to the lockups under the tower in the Loka castle and protected me from transgressions and evil!

"Let's also look," the jailer said, "at how our bishops abide! At least you will relax, because I know that what you just saw is giving you pains in the stomach."

I followed him into the castle. The high and merciful bishop, when he comes here, lives much differently than we at Visoko, who are poor and content with what God gives us in the moment. The Loka bishops, however, are high lords and it is only right that they are reserved a residence fitting for God's designated ones, which we, who dig the hard ground, are not. It would also be very unwise, because we would be carried away by vain pride when we do not have the right to be proud!

There were many gilded furnishings there and plenty of tables and chairs, large and small. Pictures hung on the walls—and not only holy ones, because the bishop, after all, was protected against every temptation—and those pictures were placed in frames that were probably more valuable than a peasant's hut. I also saw a throne on which the lord bishop sat when he received the civil and spiritual lords. And I even saw the bed where he rested after his daily labor. It was tall and wide like the tents the Israelites put up in the desert.

Here there was also a small room with three windows from which the roof of the nuns' convent was visible. A bed stood in this little room and, above it, a cross had been drawn on the wall, which indicated that something extraordinary must have taken place here.

Mihol removed the hat from his head and spoke:

"God have mercy on all the souls in Purgatory and, if it His holy will, also all the souls in hell! In this place, young man, they murdered the blessed Bishop Konrad when he was sleeping and suspecting no evil. Two servants strangled him and took five thousand silver crowns; for such high lords are, of course, never without money. But justice overtook them and they lost their heads in the neighborhood of the church at Fara. First, they cut off both of their hands and it was truly funny to see how they raised the two stumps the sickle had left them with to wipe their faces. Yes, yes, a man has it hot from the devil if something like that happens to him in life!"

And I also remember this from the jailer's speech:

"But I wouldn't want to sleep in this room, not for all of the castles that the Freising bishop has, nor if they left me a keg of holy water with which to sprinkle myself all night. The murderers haunt this place, and when the wind howls around the castle they wail from this chamber. It is no small sin to kill a bishop of our holy Catholic Church!"

That is how, on that day, Mihol Schwaiffstrighk showed me the most important secrets of the Loka castle. Later I learned that he liked to reveal these secrets to people, and that he took special pleasure when his visitors trembled with fear and terror as he led them to the underground holds and the cell where the glorified Bishop Conradus had died. So I too dragged myself back to the smithy of Master Langerholz that day, half dead and half alive, and I wished that no one should ever have anything to do with a house of repentance like the castle at Škofja Loka!

That desire was not fulfilled, at least insofar as my insignificant person, barely visible to God's sight, was concerned. I made yet other, bitter journeys to the Loka castle and I trembled for a life that, may the blessed Mother of God be my witness, was much dearer to me than my own. I crawled on my knees for that life before the most powerful. If it was saved, it was not to my credit, but to the credit of Jesus Christ, who does not allow the innocent and righteous to be abused. Therefore, He softened and opened the heart of the noble born, most magnificent, and powerful Lord Janez Frančišček, who is still today the illustrious ruler of the bishopric of Freising and all of its lands!

If God prolongs my life and prevents the carpenter—who day after day, drives nails into the funeral coffin of my wounded breast—from finishing his work for yet a few more months, I will write everything down in detail and describe it for those who come after me, that they may realize how the first rule is to have faith in God, and the second is to be meek. It is difficult for me to write—as awkward and slow as plowing land when the blade will not pierce the layer of clay. I came into the world at a time when no one in our valley from Žiri to Šefertno read books, not to mention wrote with a pen. The lord mayors and priests and the few students who attended the Ljubljana Jesuits' school were exceptions. And in Žiri—truth be told!—Jeromen Oblak, who each year traded much linen to Venice and even to German Bavaria, knew how to write, but only numbers. Yet even that served him well and brought him large profits in his distant dealings.

As for me, at the time that my hand was raising a heavy hammer above the anvil, I was also learning to write. At that time a certain acquaintance of my father was living in Loka. It was not known how old he was or where he had come from. He tanned leather for Lorenc Feguš, a Loka tanner, with whom he lived. He was a good worker. But every Sunday and holiday he would disappear from the town, and the people said that he walked in the hills and that he knew very old people there. People believed that he was not in his right mind and that he fled from the city when he became confused in his head. They called him "Tanner Valentin." Even though it was known that he did not go to church or make Easter confession, no one, not even the magistrate or Father Andrej, the parish priest, whose surname was Hudočut and who was once our priest at Poljane, paid him any attention, since he was disturbed. For the castle magistrate, Frančišček Matija Lampfrizhaimb, did not show special ardor in matters of faith, as had Lord Tomaž Chroen, the bishop of Ljubljana who partook of all the renown a man can attain on earth!

During the winter, Tanner Valentin would also teach children to become familiar with reading and writing. It was said that for a time he was even a teacher in the school of the Corpus Christi Brethren and that he had left that good place, which probably brought him a whole six gold pieces a year, because the directors insisted that he go to church now and then. I must record that Valentin beat his pupils fiercely and often dragged them by the hair. It was only with difficulty that he beat reading and writing into us with his stick.

Later, when I went out into the world, I improved my learning. Now I write with real skill, but read poorly because my eyes have tired, perhaps from a wound, perhaps from the madness that I endured in the numerous battles into which Lord Eugenius, Prince of Savoy worthy of all praise, led us.

When three years had passed, my father Polikarp in- 1676 formed me that he hoped I had learned something and that Visoko could no longer do without the labor that a lord may and must demand from his firstborn son. I returned home and began to work in the fields, the barn, and wherever I was needed. I also received all of the tools a blacksmith must have. I practiced my trade only as much as was needed on the farm: when something was in need of repair or something new had to be made, I did it, as is required in farming.

1680   At that time my brother Jurij was sent to Ljubljana to study with the Jesuit fathers. He remained in the city only four years because everyone born at Visoko has more strength in his hands than in his head and is thus happier working in the fields than sitting on a school bench. The same proved true of Jurij, and the Jesuits wrote from Ljubljana that they did not desire to keep him any longer. Father looked angry because of this and for a time he kept Jurij in real fear. But because Jurij gladly submitted to him and did any task, we were soon pleased that he had come home.

Thus God arranges everything justly!

III.

As always, father was a cruel master to me. So four years passed. During that time I noticed that I was gradually earning my father's confidence and approval. His wildness did not lessen despite his old age, something a child should really not write about a parent. When he had too much wine to drink, it was wise to get out of his way, as you would get out of the way of a vexed young bull in the pasture. And the truth is, all too often the Visoko master drank to excess.

When he approached the seventieth year of life, Polikarp Khallan began to haul wine from the Vipava country and elsewhere and trade it, because in those days, when the country had already become somewhat stronger after the German war, the people liked to have a drink; there were beer halls enough in each village that there was some alcohol to spare. Many times father would haul goods to Vipava—then we had three pairs of strong and well-equipped packhorses at Visoko—and he always brought back many vessels filled with wine.

We heard, and it became known, that the old man did not deal his goods without quarreling and fighting somewhere in the vineyards. There was even talk of serious maiming, and several times he would have fallen into the hands of the castle magistrate, Lantherij, had he not promptly settled with the injured man's kin and provided them a heavy compensation, and the magistrate a substantial bribe. Such settlements are common among us: the poor man, who has no money, goes to jail, and the rich man pays off the baron and relatives, whereupon justice, which should be the same for all, is appeased. It seems to me that such things ought not happen in the world, but because they benefited my father, I will write no more about them.

I would never ask my father what sort of adventures he had in the Vipava region, and anyway I know that he would not have told me anything about it. But it hurt me that he took my brother Jurij with him, and I was really quite frightened when I noticed that the young rascal had gotten a taste for wine in bad company and drank it like water, which is actually the healthiest drink in the world.

Thus time passed, year by year, and we lived as any farmer lives on his land, where he seldom experiences anything unusual.

It was the year 1690, in which my name-day of St. Izidor recurred for the twenty-sixth time. I had matured greatly, and I did not weaken in spirit. At least Father Karel Ignacij of Poljane frequently praised me and used me as an example for the other youths.

One Sunday afternoon when the household and family were resting, my father ordered me to come with him.

He drove me to a place we call "Osojnik," which lies below the forest and above Visoko. Just that year the beeches on Osojnik had been cut, and we had done away with the stumps by burning them, so that a fertile field was made for rye and wheat. A man cannot live on beech leaves, but he lives very nicely on the golden ears. The old man lay down on the strip of grass by the new grain field, grasped a bunch of grass, wound it up, and said to me:

"Bring a stone to bind the devil's tail, so that what we talk about won't be thwarted."

I brought a fairly heavy stone from the grain field and we placed it on the coiled grass so that infernal Satan's curled tail was covered and he could do us no harm, even if he wanted to.

Since father did not order me to lie down as well, I lacked the courage to lie down beside him. So I stood before him, on a spot where it is pleasant to look down on the Visoko property. I still recall quite vividly how we conversed, and it was quite an important conversation, because then it was revealed to me for the first time that father felt the heavy weight of his old age and that he had decided upon me as his heir at Visoko.

This is how he began:

"Tonight the black cow will calve! Careful you don't fall asleep, and the servant and maid may not sleep either! God Himself knows that you love to sleep, though each night is so long!"

When I promised him that I would not fall asleep, he groaned deeply: "I am old and sick. As long as I lived I scraped, until I had enough for this land, which today is mine and which I am so loath to let go of."

I did not answer, and he continued to lament:

"Why must a man grow old! If my backsword became dull, I sharpened it and it cut as if it had never dulled. Why can't life be sharpened like a sword, so that a man could live two hundred years, especially if he has lived in want and suffered like a beast in the yoke, only that he might gain some sod on which peacefully to lay his head in old age?! It's true! For that I suffered and even mur…"

I knew that he wanted to tell me that he had even murdered. But he did not utter the terrible word at the end. And he would not have told me anything new with it, because before this I had already guessed that the human blood he had spilt shortened his sleep during the long nights.

He moaned: "Human life is too short! The one whose tail we bound up is at fault, because he drove the first two people into sin. May his tail swell up and may he sink even deeper into the infernal sea!" He cursed in a foreign tongue I did not understand.

I humbly reminded him that cursing is sinful and forbidden by our holy Catholic faith. He looked at me arrogantly, and I was beginning to fear that he would get even angrier. Even more arrogantly, he answered me:

"A man who served in the army commanded by Gustavus Adolphus, who was present when in a certain town—the devil take the name of that town, I can't remember it—worthless officers stabbed our Wallenstein, prince and general of Friedland, to death, such a man knows best for himself what is and isn't a sin." He laughed: "The holy Catholic faith! You can't teach such a man, my fresh lad, which faith is holy and which faith is true! I know that myself!" And he repeated once more: "I know that myself!" Once more he cursed and pounded the grass beside him with his fist.

Dear Jesus! Even now he said nothing that I would not have known before. When the words "holy Catholic faith" enraged him so—that was testimony to the effect that my mother's assertion about "the Lutheran" was well grounded.

"Honor thy father!" says God's commandment. But may Saint Izidor forgive me for being silent before my father and quietly enduring the worst hurt that can touch a wretched man: I did not defend the holy Catholic faith, to which I am dedicated body and soul, with every drop of my blood!"

He would not calm down. From the rest of his talk I understood that the fear of death haunted him.

"What was death to me when we rode over the Swedes? But in old age a man doesn't want to die!" Then he added: "If I could only know that this land would stay with my people—that is what worries me!"

He looked down and scowled, and finally the words— that he wanted to will the estate to me—barely wrenched themselves from his lips. He demanded a promise from me not to dissipate, mortgage, or rent Visoko.

I promised him everything. Then he said:

"I will tell you something: Fear the Tajčars!" At that time, we called those who had been attracted to our parts from Germany and had taken the best farms from us Tajčars.

He began again: "I know that lot, they are greedy, they think they are better than us, and they are hungry

31

for our land. They tear whomever doesn't bark with them to pieces. To silence their throats I will marry you, and you will take a Tajčar, so she won't have German children. It's true they know how to work the land best. Your mother was also German-born and wasn't a bad housewife, although she liked to anger me."

He set his stare on me. "I hope you haven't hitched up your horses yet!" He watched me fixedly and with a tense face. "You will marry as I command and where I want!" Again, he spattered foreign curses about but slowly calmed down when I assured him that I had had nothing to do with any woman and that his will was mine as well.,

I did not tell him quite the whole truth. Our neighbor Debelak had a daughter who was good natured and had a nice figure. In church, when Father Karel Ignacij pronounced God's word, our eyes would occasionally search out and find each other. When we met, she would always say something pleasant, but there was nothing sinful between us.

After all this, father also revealed to me that he had already agreed with Jeremija Wulffing about his daughter Margareta from his second marriage. He added: "As soon as the wheat is harvested, you will set off with Lukež. You will take with you two fat hams and white bread so as not to arrive at Jeremija Wullfing's empty-handed. Don't say too much! Your words will be: 'My father Polikarp would like to know what and for how much can be had at Davča.' You'll bring the answer home to me. In a week we will come together at Loka, where everything will be agreed upon more exactly." He concluded: "Your mother was Jeremija's sister. It's possible that her mother— your grandmother—is still alive. It's only right that you see her. Since all of this is not yet settled, you won't ride on the road through Selce; you'll go on foot through the forests around Blegoš. I wouldn't want Visoko to be on every tongue if nothing were to come of all this!"

Thus I was sent on a journey to Davča, for a man who is to live on a farm does not have the choice of getting by without holy matrimony.

Two days later the wheat was harvested.

When two beautiful white loaves had been baked and the two of the fattest hams chosen, Lukež and I set off from home. Each of us carried a sack with a ham and a white loaf, so that we were loaded down like two pack horses. My pistol was in my belt—in those days lonely trails were nowhere safe and many iniquitous people roamed them—and Lukež strapped on a saber of the type carolers wore when they rode from village to village.

That long journey, even today, is a lively memory, and I have not yet forgotten the feelings that filled my heart.

Marriage is a necessary and quite serious matter, too. Thus it is not surprising that various thoughts, hopes, and expectations accompanied me as a young man. However, none of it came to be, and Lukež and I carried the hams and white breads to Davča without any success!

We did not have especially good luck on our journey. Right off, in Poljane, where our path went around the church, two saddled horses stood before the rectory and

Father Karel Ignacij was conversing with the sexton. Our parish was spread out and had a great challenge: besides the home church, our spiritual father had to care for sixteen missions that were scattered about the highlands. We were afraid of Father Karel Ignacij and did not like meeting him, because he was ever prepared with a stinging word.

"Where are you two going?" he asked.

Lukež, who had decorated his hat with a bright ribbon, immediately answered that we were on our way to relatives in Davča.

"So that's it," the father pastor laughed somewhat scornfully. "You're probably going after a bride?"

When we did not say anything in response, he hollered:

"Right, otherwise there won't be any order at Visoko! Your father, Izidor, and the new rectory, which is still not paid for, cause me to worry. Master Polikarp has still not returned this year's confession ticket; the one that was turned in for last year was forged. I see I'll have to report him to the bishop. Just tell him: Hudočut swallowed forged confession tickets, but Codelli won't!"

He ordered the sexton to bring the horse to the front of the church, and, as for himself, he sighed: I have to take communion to Saint Jakob's on Jarčje Hill, and it's a tough trip!"

The blood rushed to my face and I looked like a red poppy. I deeply felt the shame that I had endured because of my father's confession ticket. I knew that father did not go to Mass, but I did not know where he got the tickets every year; now Father had told me that he turned in forged tickets. What shame! And the sexton heard all of this, too, and would surely spread what he had just picked up through the whole parish, so that the Visoko household would earn a most poor reputation!

Crushed, I set off from the rectory, but fortune had it that the servant Lukež cheered me a bit with his incessant chatter. Despite his years, he trod lightly in front of me, and was happy as a lark. He knew everyone we met and every hut we passed was familiar to him. Settlements were scarce and the poor folk lived in wooden, thatched dwellings. The mountain tops, which I had never until now seen from so close, also cheered me. Much of the land was still uncultivated; where grain could have been sown, heather and ferns grew.

We made our way around Blegoš on a path that wound between thick and beautifully grown beeches. Lukež was of the opinion that a few fat bucks must be hiding in such a beechwood. Silence reigned as in a church, and only an occasional bird called from the dark treetops.

Lukež and I were not, however, alone in that solitary place! A storm had felled a beech tree just below the path and in its green branches was a man. He had placed his taught bow on his knees and he was lying in wait for any game that might happen by.

He angrily faced us; we had spoiled his hunt. His face was brown and surrounded by thick black hair, so we knew we had before us a worthless gypsy. He immediately turned his burnt face away from us again and tried to pretend that he hadn't noticed us.

Lukež, who knew everybody, also recognized this vagabond with curly black hair.

"Hoj, Dušan!" he hollered. "May God grant you and the sharp arrow in your bow luck in the hunt!"

The other turned his face to us again and a wild hatred flamed up in his black eyes. He grunted something and it seemed to me that he muttered that Lukež could blow it out of his ear or somewhere else, for all he cared. He emerged from the branches, at which my servant reached for my belt and drew my loaded pistol.

The gypsy once more took his seat in the branches and in an odd language, which they say is spoken on the Croatian border, asked whether we still had the iron chest that we put our money in at Visoko. He suggested that we keep an eye on it.

These words also frightened me, because it was a bad sign that that tramp knew about the trunk by father's bed. For those gypsies steal anything they can lay their hands on.

But Lukež shot back: "Just come, you brown devil, if you want us to sow your curly mane thick with iron beans! You black tramp, you!" With those words my servant laughed and threatened the gypsy with the pistol. But he paid no further heed to us or Lukež's imprudent talk.

During our trek we had other adventures that I did not expect because I did not imagine such secrets lay in our forests. We were already quite tired when we arrived at a small plateau, from which, deep in the valley, a village with very wonderful little white houses could be seen. Lukež maintained that the village was called Zali Log. And in truth it turned out to be Zali Log, which, however, is still a good distance from Davča.

This plateau is called "Na Svrčušah" because a vigorous cold spring that strengthens the weary and flagging traveler rushes out of the ground in its midst. And near the spring there is a tree that provides plenty of good shade.

Three women were sitting in the shade: one old one and two young ones. The latter were, without a doubt, sinners, since it was written on their faces that they would not hesitate to do anything in the world. The old one had a basket in front of her, which she clutched as if she had great treasures stored inside.

Right by the spring there was a fire, and several pots sat by the flame. We had arrived, then, at supper time, and Lukež rubbed his hands together because he found the smell from the pots quite pleasant.

There was yet another old woman in the company, who especially excited our curiosity, and about whom I have not yet said anything. She behaved very strangely— that is, I might even say, outrageously. I never set eyes on anyone like her, before or after, though I have traveled a great deal of the world and was in the wars in Italy and Hungary, where, as I have already said, our Lord Eugenius led the imperial armies.

The woman wore patched clothes and surely lived in want and poverty. But now she was leaping and dancing barefoot, her face covered with sweat and her whole body wet. Our arrival did not disturb her in the least: she danced and leapt as if for her life.

We put down our sacks and laid down on the grass. One of the younger women, who was, I judged, of gypsy stock, placed a finger on her lips for us to be quiet.

But it was getting too hot for the old woman. So she began flinging her clothes off in the middle of her leaping. With every garment she cried out: "Whose clothes are these?" The gypsy answered promptly: "Our beloved Jesus's."

I was already nervous, lest the loathsome sinner cast off her garments until she was naked; but the dance finally overcame her. Her mouth foaming and her eyes popping, she wavered, fell to the ground, and remained there as if dead.

"That woman is no stranger to me," whispered Lukež. "She is the leaper, Špela Ocepkova! In my younger years I, too, was a leaper and back then in our dances we'd often strip naked."

At that my servant turned to the old woman by the basket, who did not care very much about Špela Ocepkova's antics because she was obviously already used to such sights.

"Well, well," he addressed her, "old Pasaverica! Just look, you're still alive! Are your dealings going well?"

"Dealings?" the old woman sighed. "Dear soul, where am I to find good deals? My seventy-five years make themselves felt! What do you think? Pasaverica is no longer hard, anymore Pasaverica can barely crawl!"

"But that salve," asked Lukež, "you still probably have some of it in your basket, no?"

She began to rage and pat the basket: "Where am I supposed to get the salve? When the German war was still on, when Lord Tilly mowed down people in the field, in those days, yes, human fat was still to be had because dead men were cheaper than pears in the fall! In those days I would come to places where there was a human corpse at every step; and deserters were slaughtering even women and children, so that human fat was quite easily gotten. Dear soul, where can I get it today? These are hard times for salve dealers. God have mercy on us!"

My servant Lukež did not leave off. "You still carry some with you. Everything I'm carrying with me," she lamented, is worth almost nothing, and hardly anyone would buy such stuff. Here I have some very beautiful pictures that the bishop himself blessed in Passau. But none of this sells in your valleys. Believe me, it's become so that I often don't even have a halfpenny! And I don't have a thing today."

Here she timidly glanced at her younger companions who were mockingly laughing at her talk. Then she leaned over to me and said quietly: "I probably have something for you."

She patted her basket and drew a large package from it. "If I judge right, you're from Visoko. There's money there."

"They're confession tickets." She then added mysteriously, "they're forged but easy to pass in if you mix them with others for your family. I tell you, people are glad to buy them because it's a bother to have to run to the confessional. Perhaps you'll buy some of them—they're not too expensive."

I refused the wicked offer with great disgust because I did not want Visoko's son to come to shame like his father did. I saw that the whole company before me was depraved, worthless, and a threat to God's work.

My servant Lukež spoke up again: "At one time you were trading in linen."

"And I still do," she boasted. "From that I provide for myself and my orphaned granddaughter, who is my only consolation in old age."

She continued scornfully: "But I'm not so unwise as to carry linen about the mountains, or even the money I use to pay for it. Pasaverica is respected and everyone in the highlands knows Pasaverica. All of my trade passes through the hands of Jeromen Oblak of Žiri. What I buy is what people bring to Loka when Oblak goes there with his goods. He accepts it and pays because all of my money is kept with him. Then he takes the merchandise to the Danube, to German Passau for me. Oh no, I'm not such a cow as to carry money around in these forests!"

Here she triumphantly looked at her two younger companions, and it was perfectly obvious how avidly they drank in her words.

Then the leaper, Špela Ocepkovka, roused herself. She looked about somewhat vaguely, took a small wooden dish in her hand, poured water into it, and drank it up.

The gypsy asked curiously: "What happened?"

"What do you think happened?" Špela answered moodily.

"Nothing! My legs hurt and I have a wicked thirst—that's all."

Then she said to herself: "God is no longer with us. God has left us and the promised land is lost! I must search for a land where I can go down. There was a time when you leapt and danced until your bones cracked and you didn't think of anything but your beloved Jesus; if you swooned from the dance and lay on the ground, that dear Jesus always appeared to you. He sat on the golden clouds and silver angels sat around him. And the Lord said to us: 'Here must rise my temple!' And how we built them, the temples! A hundred and more we built, until those infernal servants, those evil bishops, came and made ashes of one roof after another for us. May dear Jesus, hand them over on Judgment Day to be whipped until bloody! When the temples were burned our dear Jesus disappeared and has not appeared ever again. Oh! Oh!"

"How is a poor woman to live after that?" she sobbed. "So I collect for the convent at Mekinje and the mother superior gave me a letter with a large seal. But no one gives anything. This country is hard and has no mercy. I will go to the Kras—there are still good people living there."

My servant Lukež teased her a little: "You probably have a bit left from when your husband was sold to the Venetian Rebecca? Don't pretend, you surely have a few ducats sewn up!"

Later Lukež explained to me that the husband of Špela Ocepkovka was condemned to prison for many years and that the high estates, who judge everything wisely, sold him to the Venetian Republic for thirty ducats. The Republic chained him aboard a galley, and he had to work the heavy oars. Thus there was a double blessing: the criminal had to work and the innocent family was paid off with as many ducats as the high estates had not taken. There are truly few lands where the inhabitants are so cared for as our Carniolian landed gentry, who will not escape heaven's retribution!

But the Venetian ducats badly incensed Ocepkova. "You dog, you!" she screamed. "You bark at me when I haven't done anything to you! You mangy dog, you! I'm old but I hope that I still live to see the day when they drag you to Gavžnik and hang you! If God grants it, they'll first cut off your hand and then cut out your devilish tongue!"

"Lukež went pale at the old witch's hollering. He answered somewhat hollowly: "Just yell, I'm not at all afraid of you, you mother of the devil! When you perish, we'll take care to drive a stake through you before we bury you outside the fence! Then just see how you'll get out of the grave, you disgusting hag!"

"Sooner than you think," the Špela fumed, "the worms will be eating you, big white worms, because you attacked a maiden of the true God!"

Then she turned to me with a nice word: "You're sensible! You'll be a good master at Visoko and you'll earn a great deal. Your sack is wide and stuffed. Perhaps you have some brandy in it? Treat me to a couple of swallows!"

We actually did have brandy with us, and, so as not to earn her wrath, I poured her some in the wooden bowl from which she had drunk water. I filled the bowl almost halfway with the burning drink. And then I was amazed at how deftly and in one gulp she drank down the brandy I had poured. I knew right away that she had drunk a lot of it during her lifetime.

She thanked me and called down upon me all of the blessings of the glorified leapers who had once raised temples on the earth and danced in honor of dear Jesus.

And what could I do? Lukež, however, had a nasty look on his face because he himself did not shun brandy. But such a woman, who surely had ties to the devil, could have harmed us greatly if she were to have cast a spell on our pregnant cow, for instance, or sent black clouds and hail upon us, which would destroy everything that had been planted.

God forbid that I say a word against the authorities established for us by Him! They care for us well; however, I cannot be silent and I must say that they mind such evil old women, who are in league with the devil and of whom there are more in the world than we think, too little. If our eyes would be opened some night, we would see many women we know among them when they ride around in the sky. You say a star fell. But it is not so. It is a woman who has not become accustomed to her work falling from her broom, but before she hits the ground, Satan catches her, so that she does not break her bones.

That was my conviction on that day when I poured the leaper Špela Ocepkova some brandy.

The Lord Jesus was not pleased with that conviction and, in his justness, sent a bitter and piercing punishment upon me.

Just as the leaper had flagged earlier after her dance, she now flagged after the drink. She fell asleep.

Immediately her two younger companions were about her and with great dexterity they felt her skirt and all the parts of her poor clothing in which some money could have been sewn. But they did not come upon anything because Lukež's words had been empty and spoken in haste.

The gypsy woman accused Lukež of lying when he prattled about the ducats that were supposedly sewn into the leaper's clothes. Since she had not discovered anything, she wanted to earn some money another way. She turned to my servant with the words: "Pay a soldo and I'll read your palm!"

A soldo was a lot of money for Lukež and he didn't like to pay it even at dances. So he begged: "Izidor, pay! It's not safe to refuse such devilish women anything."

I was overcome by sinful curiosity, so I paid the woman two soldos so she would also tell my fortune.

She looked first at Lukež's hand and ran her fingers over his palm. "Brother," she cried, "you have waded deeply in blood, and it's amazing you didn't drown in it; there is also the blood of women and children."

Lukež retorted: "What are you prattling about? Everyone in our valley knows that Polikarp and I were in the German war. Every kid knows that we weren't picking flowers there. And *you* didn't know that?"

The woman did not release his hand but studied his palm more intensely. Finally, she said solemnly: "Don't fire, brother, don't fire, no matter how hard they bang on the door! Don't fire, so as not to shoot yourself!"

My servant pulled his hand away and grumbled, "What am I to shoot with? An old musket is hanging upstairs that hasn't been loaded in ten years. I'm not so stupid as to use it! Get out of here!"

The gypsy gave a lively laugh and reached for my hand.

She also measured the lines on my palms with her fingers and said: "Poor fellow, your hand is covered with human blood, although you yourself didn't spill it. But you will do penance for that blood and not one of your wishes will be fulfilled on this earth! The road you are traveling today is in vain."

I am not in a condition to describe how my heart beat, because, even before, I sensed in my soul that I would do penance for my father's sins!

The gypsy noticed that I was downcast. Since she was happy with my fear, she added: "You will die, and when you are dying your body will be shot through."

Then one of her companions called: "Our husband is coming!" So, these two ugly creatures had one husband between them!

The gypsy Dušan, whom we had disturbed during his hunt, stepped out of the green bushes. He carried a young buck he had managed to surprise in the quiet forest.

The husband with two wives threw his catch on the grass; an arrow was sticking into the animal's neck. He did not look at us. He laid down on the ground and cried out: "Eat!"

Both his wives, the gypsy and the other one—later I learned that she was the daughter of a good landowner in the Selška valley and that the other woman and the gypsy had lured her from the home of her respected father—were instantly all humility and obligingness.

The gypsy woman fawned: "First something special! But I beg you, Dušan, don't be angry if it's not good!" She added: "I was thinking of you when I stole it."

"Go to the devil!" muttered Dušan. She, too, lost her temper and answered angrily: "You can leave it if you don't like it! Don't you dare lay a hand on me; if you do, I'll defend myself!"

Then she continued: "That Felenič, who says Mass in Selce, who knows everything—who cures people and young pigs, who can speak with a calf inside a cow—got from Germany or God knows where some sort of new turnip, and he says it's the best fruit God created. He planted long rows of this vegetable in the garden where we stole his rooster in the spring. Last night I pulled up several rows and today I cooked this new food, dear Dušan!"

"Go to the devil!" was again the gypsy's reply.

The gypsy woman silently poured the new food from the pot that she had taken off the fire a while ago into a dish and put it all in front of her swarthy husband. As far as I could tell, the dish was something similar to the acorns that grow on our oaks onto the plate, only a bit thicker and not so brown.

The gypsy Dušan filled his mouth but at the same time yelled loudly, either because the food was too hot or had a foul taste. He kicked at the pot, overturning it so that the acorns flew out in all directions. Some of them flew over to where we were lying, and Lukež grabbed two or three because he was driven by the curiosity that at that time ailed the Poljane men and women. An uproar ensued. The gypsy jumped up in anger, but at that moment his wives armed themselves with clubs. If a fight were to break out then, Dušan probably would have tamed his womenfolk, but certainly a few hot ones would have fallen upon his brown hide as well!

But the two of us did not wait. Instead, we took our sacks and hurried along the path with quick steps. We were already a good distance from the sinful group when we caught our breath and rested a little.

"What do you think, wouldn't it be all right if we tried the pastor's turnip too?" In his open palm, Lukež offered me three acorns that he had carried off from the gypsy.

I took one. "Why not, after all it grew on Christian soil." But the morsel was bland, without any taste, and a thin skin stuck to it that was unpleasant in your teeth, so we were happy when we managed to get it all out of our mouths. We determined that Father Felenič would not save the Selška valley with that new turnip!

IV.

We walked yet a long while in the terrible heat and drank heartily from the springs that frequently crossed our path. Here and there we met with a beggar or came upon a shepherd watching his small livestock. We asked if we were on the right path, since we could have easily gone astray. The afternoon was already half over when we arrived at a manor house surrounded by nicely cultivated land.

It was here that Jeremija Wulffing had settled and made himself a new home; surely he worked diligently and hard, because he had to turn a good deal of earth. He built himself a new house that stood out handsomely among the huts that were to be seen in those hills. The house, though wooden, was quite a bit higher than the houses in our valley. When entering, you did not have to bend over to avoid knocking your head against the ceiling, and you could breathe quite freely, since there was enough fresh air in the dwelling.

At first we thought no one was home. But then we noticed an old woman sitting at the large table, completely bent over, with her face all wrinkled up, and otherwise just skin and bones! Occasionally she waved a limp hand at the bothersome flies. She uttered several words which I could not understand because German speech is like a wheel creaking haltingly over sharp stones.

Lukež, who was more knowledgeable about that clumsy language, told me the woman at the table wanted to know who we were.

When we had put our sacks down by the stove, I stepped to the table, where the old woman began telling me that no one was home and everyone was in the fields.

"We're from Visoko," I hollered, for it seemed to me that the old gal was deaf as well.

She looked at me blankly and repeated: "From Visoko!" She pondered. "Where's that, my God, where's that?"

"He's the son," Lukež bellowed, "of Polikarp and his wife Barbara."

This triggered her memory somewhat and she began slowly:

"Barbara …! I had a daughter and Barbara was her name. She renounced the holy gospel and from that time she was no longer my daughter. I cast her from my heart like weeds from the grain field. She was afraid of the murderous castle servants—she is my daughter no more! Don't speak to me of Barbara!"

She spoke haltingly. Between pauses, she thought carefully and the words dripped from her the way water drips from the channel when the spring dries up in the summer.

Lukež pointed at me and yelled: "He's your Barbara's son!"

"Her son?" she sighed. "Sit down here so I can see you close up, for my eyes are like candles that are burning down. 'The light of my eyes—it also has gone from me!'" she complained as in the psalm.

I sat down next to her in the corner and for a while she touched my face with her hand and observed me.

Finally she sobbed: "It's true, he has her face!" Then she asked sharply: "Do you acknowledge the pure gospel?"

I answered that I did not.

"Then you're a papist! I don't have a daughter and her son is dead to me too! The springs of the pure gospel are dwindling in this unhappy land and the people draw water from a puddle in which the rot of Babylon collects! It's time, Lord, that you called me from the earth, because my heavy head is bowed deeplyupon my chest!" Then she whispered: "Her son is here but he has come to me like a stranger. This affliction should have passed me by too! Let it end now! Call Trubar!"

She spoke more and more sleepily until her head dropped. And in truth she had fallen asleep, for the flies were able to land undisturbed on her limp skin.

So for the first time I saw my grandmother and my bitterness was multiplied because she was a heretic, as was master Polikarp of Visoko.

It got extremely hot in the room and the flies were also becoming oppressive. On a bench by the door stood a bucket, but there was no water in it with which I could slake my thirst. Therefore I took the dipper from the bucket and went into the hall. It seemed to me that there was water running at the back door. I stepped into a clearing, where there was indeed water running down a long channel.

A girl was standing by the channel and she was washing rags in a little tub. She had not yet turned around, thinking that one of her own was coming.

I took out the dipper and with that the girl noticed that I was a stranger. She stepped back a little and stared at me intently, as if she were an image in an altar. In a moment the blood rushed to the skin of her white neck—she had not dressed especially carefully for washing—and perhaps to her cheeks too, but I do not know exactly, because her face was burned and dark from working in the sun. I drank from the dipper and directed my gaze toward her for a moment. Her eyes were still fixed on my face. And now it seemed to me that all of the blood had left her neck and a sort of timidity filled her look. But she still did not remove her eyes from my face.

Putting aside the dipper, I said: "Now you can have a good look at me, Margareta!"

She took a step back and answered uncertainly: "You know my name?"

"My father spoke of you."

"Then you're a Visokan? My father spoke of you too." She again brightened around the neck, and I recalled mornings when the dawn lies over the mountains.

She stepped to the tub and set about doing the wash. When she could, she glanced over to the spot where I was standing. She was the type of girl who is usually pleasing to a man: well grown and prepared for any work. But the words of the gypsy—that I would make today's trip in vain and that I would die from a gunshot to the chest—would not allow me to really appreciate the body of the girl my father had chosen to become my bride. I was also tormented by an awareness that there was Lutheranism in the house, and that marriages in such houses do not partake of God's blessing, as the marriage in the Visoko house did not partake of it either.

Because I had to say something, I asked if the tithe was burdensome and high and how life was for them.

"We live in the hills," she answered, "and our life is hard! I can't complain, father is good and treats us well. But my two brothers are rough men and rude to their mother, making it worse for her than for women in other houses. I can't complain, yet there are times I would rather live in another place, among other people!"

She told me this and I could see that she wanted to leave the place that was home to her, and that she was probably pleased I had come. She finished her work, dried her hands on her apron, and called to me:

"Father is probably already here by now!"

And, indeed, we met an elderly man of tall, bony build in the house and—something of a rarity among us—with marvelous blue eyes. Lukež had placed the offerings from Visoko on the table before him: two hams and two golden loaves of bread.

While I had been lingering outside by the spring, the old woman had crawled up on the stove and from there she observed the goings on by the table. She probably guessed what the gifts meant and railed crossly:

"Don't give her to the papist, Jeremija! Jesus, don't give her to the papist, for you know that my blood flowed out for the holy gospel!"

He stepped to the bench and caressed her flaccid little face with his large hand, saying: "Quiet, mother!"

She was immediately calmed down. And my soul was also soothed and I felt very good, because that blue-eyed man showed respect for God's Fourth Commandment, even though she who had born him was of the Lutheran faith! I resolved that I would like to pay my old father homage always, even though he did not go to Mass or Holy Communion!

Then Jeremija came up to me, made a big sign of the cross over my face and said: "So at last you have come to your relatives!"

Then another woman approached, who had until then been sitting on a bench by the hearth, so that I had not noticed her. She also made the sign of the cross over my face and then silently returned to the hearth.

She was the lady of the house, and one could see by looking at her that she was overwhelmed by constant work, and everything about her said that her life was a tasteless and bland food, as any woman must experience who takes on a widower and his children.

The father and I sat down at the table on which Margareta had put a large loaf, and she was not satisfied until I had cut a piece. Then she disappeared into the hall to prepare supper.

The rest of us studiously avoided any word that was in the least connected with my purpose in coming to this house. For the most part, we talked about the after-grass, the cutting of which was to begin the next day.

A clamor was heard in the hall. There followed some talk with Margareta, at which point the doors quickly opened. The two sons, the elder Marks and the younger Othinrih, burst into the room; I do not know how the latter came by such an inhuman name. They were like two angry hornets. They came up to their father, but did not yet look at me.

Marks spoke up first: "What is it, father? What's this Margareta is telling us?"

And Othinrih banged the table and hollered: "… and you want to send her from our house when you know that we two couldn't live without her!"

Marks became even angrier: "And she is to go to people who talk like our dogs bark!" Marks, too, pounded the table with his fist.

The indecent nonsense about my native language incensed me and I wanted to say something to those boys that they would not like. But Margareta hurried into the room, took Othinrih by the sleeve and dragged him after her, pleading with both of them to calm down and not to aggravate their father, who angered easily and became enraged over every trifle.

"We don't want you to be sold from our house!" they yelled. But they left off nonetheless because their half-sister had more power over them than I expected.

The master of the house did not become angry, although a spark appeared in his blue eyes. The woman on the stove also spoke up once more and I heard how she sighed:

"Jeremija, why are you forcing her out of the house? You love her and your sons love her, though you didn't bring them up as is commanded in God's book. Wait a while! Surely a Christian youth will come who will want to have her, who will woo her as Jacob wooed his wife. If he isn't from here, he will come from somewhere else, from Germany, where they who acknowledge the holy gospel are victorious. Trubar will find him for you. Trubar, from whose lips comes the pure word of God, as sweet as honey from the hive!"

Jeremija was immediately by her side again, and again he put his hand on her wrinkled face: "Quiet, mother! If someone were to report you to the castle magistrate, they would clamp you in chains and you would have to die in the dungeons of the Loka castle!"

Then the old woman raised her voice so that her words were heard through the entire room:

"The Lord could not bestow a greater joy on me than if what you said would come true! To bear witness to the gospel would be my joy, though they cover all the limbs of my sinful body with chains! You refused to witness and Barbara didn't bear witness, because for you two, the good things of this world were more important than the blessings of the heavenly kingdom! And the knowledge that the children born of my flesh have forsaken what is most holy lies upon me like a rock, so that my tormented soul cannot escape my body, which long ago I should have given up to the black earth! Call Trubar!"

Then she sighed: "For behold, the days are coming when I will say: 'Blessed are the barren and the wombs that never bore, and the breasts that never gave suck!' I am the dried grass on the roof and I became dry before I was uprooted. My soul's hope rests in the Lord, and in Him do I trust, that the tears may be dried from my eyes. The lips of my neighbors do not proclaim the truth and they do not give refreshment. I hurry to the kingdom of the living, where the Lord keeps his treasures. Day and night, suffering is my nourishment. The Lord has sent a great water upon me that I may drown it. My soul was persecuted and my life pounded into the ground!"

She sprawled on the stove and probably fell asleep because she did not speak another word that evening.

After supper, during which nothing of note occurred—only the brothers Marks and Othinrih looked angry, without uttering a single word—they took us to a small room, where Lukež and I were shown a wide bed on which both of us could easily spend the night. We quickly fell asleep after our long walk and slept very well until early morning. Just after dawn, I rose and had a look about Wulffing's farm.

There was quite a bit of livestock in the barn and, I must say, it was no worse than ours at Visoko; perhaps a little worse, but surely not much, even though my father Polikarp was reputed to know how to handle cattle.

I threw some fodder into the creche. When Marks and Othinrih got up a good while later, everything was done. I ignored the laughter and harsh words; but Margareta, who came to milk, and her father, who came for us, liked my work.

Othinrih saddled a horse and rode off towards Zali Log for the entire morning in order to get some sweet wine. There was some talk about Črni Kal wine; but it was surely not to be had in Zali Log, because even the Loka bishops could not always get it, either because the grapes yielded too little or because Črni Kal was also too expensive for a bishop.

The whole morning we cut the aftergrass, while the master asked me about our own estate. He wanted to know how many measures of wheat and other grains we harvested, how many head of livestock we had in the barn, and how many horses we had for hauling. My answers pleased him well because he became more talkative with each one. As for myself, I kept remarking that at Visoko we cut better and more aftergrass.

In the afternoon we ate a lot. The lady baked a ham we had brought along and enough of everything else. I wondered at the thick dumplings filled with cheese and walnuts, which I had never before eaten.

Grandmother did not come down from the stove to show herself, but the lord brought some of every dish to her. He also brought her some white bread, and it was clear to me that the little old woman still very much had her strength and ate quite a quantity of food for her age.

Margareta and her mother were in holiday dress. If I am not mistaken, her father was also more handsomely dressed than on the previous evening.

Only Marks and Othinrih came to the table in the worst clothing and ate for four others, so that the Visoko ham disappeared into the bottomless stomachs of the Wulffing sons in enormous pieces. We cut the white bread and drank Črni Kal wine from Zali Log, which in my opinion, though, was some Vipava wine mixed with a poor Istrian.

We had our fill of food and drink. We waited for a conversation to begin about the mission on which we had come from Visoko with gifts, and in recognition of which the hard-working lady had prepared a good and filling dinner. As was his duty, Lukež, who had come with me and who had wound a colorful ribbon around his hat according to the custom of suitors in those days, began the conversation.

"It will be time," with these words my servant turned towards me, "it will be time for us to be going! It will be a long journey and, if all goes well, we will be home by midnight. It tires a man to travel in the dark and, what's more, through the forest."

Jeremija Wulffing nodded and then set his gaze upon me as if it were my turn to say something. Margareta gathered up the dishes and spoons and hurried from the room.

The words did not come easily to me. Who would not be embarrassed when asked to say before the gathered family that he has chosen their own daughter for his wife, and especially if the suitor and his bride had never seen one another before that day?

But I managed to say: "Father ordered me to come to you and ask if you would care to answer to that about which you and he spoke on St. Jakob's day in Loka."

At this question of mine the mother and sons at the table became attentive, because everyone knew that something important for the whole house would be decided.

Father Jeremija answered thus:

"You know how to work, you rise early, you aren't wont to quarrel, as I saw yesterday, and you are deserving of praise. Neither is Margareta afraid of work. The language you talk your house does not come easily to her, but she will become accustomed to it, because a lady is always guided by her master. There are two of you at Visoko, and Polikarp will be able to give both of you much. I have a few more, but they will not leave my house empty-handed. So then! Bring your father this answer: 'Two hundred Venetian ducats, to which I will add another hundred Venetian crowns.' That is my answer!"

The offer was in all regards respectable and satisfactory. The heir who was to assume the two Visoko holdings could not count on a wealthier bride. However, my servant Lukež blurted out unnecessarily: "And a few more measures of grain too!" With that the fire that had been smoldering beneath that roof burst forth and in an instant a tall flame appeared.

Jeremija, somewhat stung, nevertheless answered coolly: "What I have spoken, I have spoken!" but his two sons roared with one voice:

"Two hundred ducats and another hundred Venetian crowns!" They rose like cornered bears and pounded the table with their fists, so that the tableware which Margareta had not already taken with her rattled.

"Two hundred Venetian ducats!" bellowed Othinrih. "All of our poverty is not worth much more!"

"And on top of that a hundred Venetian crowns!" yelled Marks. "The last head in the barn will have to be sold, and the two of us can go begging or join the gypsies on Blegoš!" Here Marks grabbed a plate from the table and hurled it out the door of the room, breaking it into pieces.

Jeremija Wulffing only paled and still said nothing. But Margareta's mother could not remain silent and said tearfully:

"But we two have also worked hard! Margareta and I have never sat with our arms folded!"

I would almost think that the two sons were just waiting to set upon their stepmother, who looked like a heap of housewifely poverty. "You just be quiet!" they bellowed, and poked her in the crude mountain way, as if she were the lowest servant girl on the farm.

"Not even a word from you!" cried Marks. "What did you bring to this house?"

Othinrih roared with laughter. "What every woman brings to a house!" They beat on the table again, and Jeremija Wulffing remained silent. It was a wonder that he did nothing to protect his second wife, who simply shrank before her two stepsons' dispute.

The two of them could not calm themselves; on the contrary, they rushed from one outrage to another. And they were so blinded by it that they also attacked their own parent and master.

"What will you give us when up to now we have had nothing good?" they yelled. "We were the oxen of the house and always in the yoke!"

"You slept," the older one laughed at him, "yet everything was always done."

"You never worked very much," added the younger, "even when we mowed and threshed."

All of the features on father Jeremija's face began to contort. He was a man who did not like to be excited, but he became angry when pricked in the most sensitive place, when he was told what he least liked to hear about his life, but that too his callous sons told him on that day.

"If you think of it," Marks spoke, "almost everything was mother's, and only a little bit of it was yours."

"Mother," hissed Othinrih, "liked to say: 'When I took your father he had nothing but what he could carry on his back.'"

The two of them roared devilishly. Marks added: "It would be best for us to put a red rooster on the roof! Then we'll get the Venetian crowns, when we know where they are!"

And Othinrih said: "Then you'll have as much as when our mother took you.!"

So those two fools attacked their own father, to whom they owed obedience and love!

Jeremija Wulffing rose from his place in a flash, reached for the holy images, and drew from behind them a long, thick birch rod of the type one takes into the field to drive lazy cattle along.

Then the sons became timid and hurried from the table to save their skins from the blows. But the old man caught up with them at the door to the room and they were not able to escape. The birch rod sang its loud song, snapping on their backs, heads and arms, wherever it struck and fell. Father Wulffing did not utter the slightest word while doing this, he simply beat them.

Amidst the noise a tiny voice was heard, thin and ragged, just as if it came from deep in the earth, as if you heard it in a dream or when drowsing. At the stove, grandmother was singing:

Ach Jesu! lass michsehen
Dich / O du schoenesLiecht:
Hoer an mein Bitt und Flehen /
Zeig mir deinAngesicht!
Moecht bald ich zudirfahren /
Wie gern ich sterbenwolt!
Kein Gelt / keingute Jahren /
Kein Freuntmichthaltensolt.

Immediately the house became quiet. The boys disappeared and the father once again stuck his virtuous birch rod behind the icons. In my heart I wondered at those Germans, that they thus bring up their children, beating them, even if they are grown and the chief laborers in the house. At Poljane it would be hard to find a young fellow twenty years old who would not forcibly stop his old father, if he had the mind to, from humiliating him before strangers and speaking to him with a birch rod.

Jeremija Wulffing said: "So then! What I said has been decided! In two weeks will be the feast of St. Ahac. Tell your father that on that day we will go to Loka. The castle scribe or the town recorder—the second is cheaper—will record what must be recorded, that all may be in right and lawful order!"

We conversed about this and that, and then Lukež and I set out.

And our travel was easier because the sacks were empty. We had already walked several thousand paces, so that only a small piece of roof on one of Wulffing's buildings was yet visible. We reached the place where

the path heads downhill. There on the slope sat Jeremija's sons. They were waiting for us, and in a quite ag-
gravated mood; however, they did not have any weapons in hand, the way our young men usually fought.
They got up, and immediately I noticed that their father's switch had left its mark. Red threads ran across
their faces and their arms too.

Othinrih, who was bolder than his brother, stepped
up to me and said: "So you think that we Davča boys
are sheep anyone can beat up!"

"That's what you'll say over your whole dirty valley!"
Marks added.

Then they joked about our language again and once
more mentioned dogs, saying that they speak better than
we, who are supposedly baptized at God's altar. They
spoke with great contempt, and this mockery of our language seemed to me very wrong, when, if you had to listen to the two of them, they themselves used words that
made you feel as if you were swallowing broken glass.

I overcame my anger and obeyed my good sense,
which told me that it was not worth quarreling, or even
fighting with those two, who were my cousins by my
mother and my half-brothers by my bride. I also tamed
Lukež with my gazes. We tried to pass by them in silence, which provoked them even more.

Othinrih stood in my path and asked: "Do you have
anything in your pants, you Carniolian worm? That's
what I'd like to know!"

Marks wanted to know the same thing, and Lukež
grumbled something about it being more than the two
of them could handle.

Othinrih kept demanding that I fight with him. Marks wanted at least to wrestle, if I did not have the courage to fight with them. He insisted that I must have some strength in me if—after all, I was marrying and would no longer sit before a bowl my mother poured milk into.

The talk was becoming ever more stinging. Lukež put aside his sack, shed his jacket and rolled up his sleeves. He had already spit into his fist and made a sign that he was ever ready to take part in a fight, as befitted a one-time *cuirassier*, be he was already seventy years old. The danger threatened that we would tangle, either fighting or wrestling.

Our beloved Lady of Malenski Mountain hurried to our aid. That is, just as the quarrel was beginning, my betrothed, Margareta, arrived. In a moment she recognized that we were going to fight, because she knew her brothers' arrogance and rashness well. She reprimanded them and sent them off with a sharp word. And I write the pure truth when I say that Marks and Othinrih lost all their courage and took fright of their sister, as previously they had of their father! And I will add: when she was angry like that, when she was ordering her brothers around, she was pretty and pleasing to my eyes!

She walked on with us for a while, probably to prevent her brothers from returning and looking for another quarrel. When she was sure that the danger had been avoided, she stopped and took a small bundle from somewhere in her clothing. Again, the blood filled her white neck and she timidly searched for words to say to me. As you know, father Jeremija had stressed that the language of my native country did not come easily to her;

Margareta wanted to show, at our parting, that that language was not strange to her. She offered me the bundle, confused some of our words and ended pleadingly: "Nehmi, Nehmi!"

I took it and she hurried off. When I opened the bundle there was a piece of white bread, and it was wrapped in a little kerchief like the ones brides give to their suitors, according to the adopted Italian custom.

The humbly spoken "nehmi" rang in my ears for a long time, even after Lukež had explained to me that the Tajčars on the Sora plain blend their language in just the same way, fitting their own German words to our language.

On the remainder of our journey, we experienced nothing worth noting here. We went along the same path as before, when we came from Visoko. There was no trace of anyone at Svrčuše. Only a black spot remained by the spring where the gypsies had cooked. There was not a voice to be heard in the whole forest and anyone who would have lain down on the ground would have fallen asleep.

We had passed Blegoš when there was a great crashing noise high above us in the great forest, as if a cut tree trunk were falling to the ground. We stopped, gazing in wonder at what it might be. The disturbance spread all along the mountainside until, like a shot above us through the thicket, roared a deer, a giant stag. He hung in the air with his antlers, which were as long as a long broom, laid over his back.

"Did you see him?" wondered Lukež. "If I had my musket with me, I would have shot him, and he would have fallen in the clearing! Oh, that was a sight!"

He immediately cooled off when I answered: "What if Bishop Albreht Sigismund had found out? He would show you what it means to shoot at his deer!"

"Those high lords," complained Lukež, "retain for themselves everything that is of any worth and offer us paupers the worst! The devil take them!"

He told me about the deceased Bishop Vid Adam, who, to the dismay of the Loka subjects, sat on the bishop's throne for many years. He was a severe ruler. Each day he craved a higher tithe and all the days of his rule he litigated with his subjects, so that once they even had to carry their parchment to German Gradec, then again to Vienna, and once even to the emperor in Regenspurk, or whatever that damned German town is called. They accomplished nothing because it was, and always will be, thus: that the emperor does not peck out the eyes of a bishop nor of the least lord! And neither will his successor, Albreht Sigismund, be much better, as the subjects in Železniki have already concluded. Seven of them banded together to kill some deer. And is that anything special? But the bishop sentenced all of them to pay one hundred and twenty thaler. Since when is a deer worth that much! Yet they had to pay if they did not want to go to Mihol Schwaiffstrigkh, who provides only poor drink and poor quarters!

Thus we conversed until we were once again at Visoko, where father Polikarp was very happy to receive news of Jeremija Wulffing's answer. Neither do I want to conceal that that night I dreamt of Margareta, his daughter.

V.

God guides the events of this world in His own way, and only that happens which His almighty will desires!

The feast of St. Ahac approached, and father was preparing to hand his property over to me. During that time he spoke with me more than usual and gave me instructions for the future. He gave me directions on farming and the wine trade—especially to avoid our money when selling, because it was quite a bit less valuable than the German coin. And best of all is Venetian coin! That I should not heed provocations against the estate, and that, if that "voivode" Jernac Schiffrer were to come, I show him the door, for the claims the voivode lodges on the peasants' behalf only take money from the house and bring in nothing! How much sweet wine had the litigants shipped off to Gradec, and the lords drank the wine, but it was the bishop who received his justice, which a sensible man should have foreseen! Thus it was that father instructed me; but later God arranged everything differently.

After we returned from Davča, and when, one time, Lukež had recounted the story of the gypsy who had asked about the iron chest at Visoko, father listened very attentively and ground his teeth a few times. He could not get the gypsy's question out of his mind and, like a good warrior, arranged everything so that the enemy would not surprise him with an unexpected attack. We put strong new bolts on the front and back doors. Father abandoned the cellar and moved into the upper house with his chest. Lukež and I likewise had to go upstairs, and, to avoid confusion, we kept a loaded musket at hand every night. The women slept downstairs, and the oxman and shepherd in the barn, because we did not anticipate that anyone would attempt a break-in against the livestock or cattle. The latter did not have much value anyway, and thus we were not concerned that there were a few head more or less at our house. As for myself, I was not expecting anything bad because no robberies had been heard of for a long time. Neither was there any news from the highlands. Therefore, I was convinced that father's worries were exaggerated and overblown.

But after midnight, several days before the feast of St. Ahac, we were awakened by a noise in front of the house. Some of them were scurrying around the farmhouse, and some were beating on the front doors, demanding that Polikarp hand over his war chest if he did not want them to break into the house by force.

We all got up, even the women on the ground floor. The latter called for people to help and caused a tumult that was probably heard as far as Log. Father hurried to us with a bared sword in his hand. He placed Lukež by the window to guard the barn and back door. Jurij and I had to go to the front window so as not to leave the main entrance unguarded.

The robbers negotiated a little while longer but the negotiations came to nothing because the lord of the house would have rather lost his life than parted with the iron chest and the money in it. He raged until he frothed when the oxman yelled from the barn that they had gotten into the sheep shed, which was not locked tightly. And, indeed, they dragged two of the best sheep out and drove them into the woods that surround St. Sobota.

They beat on the front door a while longer but achieved nothing, because it was iron plated. Then they chose the back door, which was weaker and more readily broken into. Four men dragged a heavy log from somewhere and rammed the door with it until the bolt was about to release. We were already afraid that it would do so when father grabbed the musket from my hands and, without aiming, fired at those at the door. No one was hit, but the thunder rolled through the valley. Already voices could be heard coming from the village. A light appeared in the house of our neighbor, Debelak, and the sexton at St. Volnik's was already pulling on the bell, raising a hue and cry, as is done in case of fire.

The robbers quit and had to think of escaping and getting to safety. They darted about like shadows and one nimbly stepped up to the fire those shameless beings had set in the yard. He grabbed a burning stick and hurried with it to a place where the barn's thatched roof was so low that he could shove his torch into it.

"That devil is offering us a red rooster," hissed Lukež between his teeth. "The Swedes also had that ugly habit." He rested his heavy musket against the wall and took distant aim with it. When the iron struck the flint, spraying sparks into the gunpowder, the arsonist was knocked down by the explosion; he rolled on the ground and the stick flew away before he could shove it into the straw. Poor Lukež was trapped by his former military pride! He waved his hand in the moonlight in front of the open window and yelled: "Vivat! Victoria!"

Something black flew in. Below, the bandits gathered up the man who was writhing on the ground and carried him off, while Lukež collapsed at the window. A thin arrow was stuck deep in his chest just above the heart.

The neighbors approached noisily, but no one dared to go into the forest after the robbers. They only made a clamor and talked, and were of no use.

Father and I took looked after Lukež, who was in need of human and heavenly help. We wanted to carry him to a bed, but he wished to lie on the floorboards; we only shoved a few rags under his head so that he could breathe more easily. He was fully conscious and asked father to sit down on the stool by his head.

"Polikarp, comrade," he said, "send for the priest, my time is short!"

Brother Jurij saddled a horse and hurried off to the Poljane chaplain. The mortally wounded man continued: "Polikarp, comrade, do you still remember how Friedland grouped us in the field near German Lützen? Our ranks stood behind a deep trench; there were a few infantry in front, then we were in the saddle. Hah, we were an iron wall, we Pappenheim cavalrymen! Hah, it was beautiful and those were wonderful times!

Of course, you still remember how Gustavus Adolphus himself then roared and the earth shook?! Whatever they say, he was a great captain, that Gustavus Adolphus, and he was skilled at war like few others! Do you still remember all of that? He was across the trench like a bullet with the heavy cavalry, and our infantry was stomped into the ground. But he thought that there would be more of them. And we on horseback were very close, because that is what our Duke Pappenheim had decided. They came down on us. We two and Pečarjev Boltežar from Gabrška Mountain were in the first rank and immediately fired our muskets at the Swedish king. He flinched slightly and the wide hat with white feathers disappeared from his head. And you yelled: 'Look, Lukež, what a big and heavy gold chain he has around his neck!' Well, one of the filthy infantrymen who had saved himself from beneath the hooves of the Swedish horses shot him in the back from behind and knocked him from the saddle. And we were over him like a storm, so that later they barely wrested him away from the pile of corpses. But we didn't get the gold chain and only God knows what devils took it from us, for it should have belonged to us, because Gustavus Adolphus was first hit by our muskets! Such fighting was glorious and it would have been easier for me to die in that battle! But our Duke Pappenheim, a good but harsh commander, also fell! Even now tears come to my eyes when I remember that famous captain! O, my dear one, you too remember all of it because something like that cannot be forgotten!"

At these words father became agitated and walked back and forth across the room. Lukež fell silent for a moment, then began again:

"Pečarjev Boltežar! Look, he, too, was shot through and through in the battle at Emmerhausen, where we pounded the Swedes! When he lay on the grass he said: 'I thought that there were more steps to the heavenly kingdom, but you go up very quickly!'" Lukež strained to laugh but it was difficult for him, because he himself was at the steps to the heavenly kingdom.

He called the Visokan over. "Polikarp, comarade! I see now that it's nothing to die; but before I die I would like to know something! God only knows if Jošt Schwarzkobler, the one with whom we rode for so many years through the fields and villages of Germany, is still alive? Only God knows if he is still alive!"

Father stopped by the wounded man and I noticed how his knees shook when he sat down on the stool. "Schwarzkobler...! He's probably still alive... why wouldn't he be?"

Lukež fell silent and thought for a while.

The lord spoke up: "Lukež, don't take offense! You know that, because of that treasure we got at Emmershausen and took from the Swedish baggage, I didn't tell you everything. I hid your share from you and falsely said Schwarzkobler took your portion by force! It is still with me and I will pay it out to you when you get well!"

With what difficulty those words came from his mouth! Surely he was very troubled that he had to admit something like that in the presence of his son!

However, this news did not shake the wounded man. He answered calmly: "Polikarp, comrade! Why are you telling me such things! You were my friend for all the days we knew each other, but I depended on you like a dog on his master because you had much more sense and a better head. I was satisfied that I was allowed to come here to Visoko and allowed to live with you. And now, when my last hour is come, you should be thanked! You were my lord, but you were also my friend; you gave me to eat and drink. Did I ask for anything more?"

Here he began about running the farm: "Polikarp, the Posavčeva girl, who is now a little servant with you, will amount to nothing. You will have to send her off... Do not sow wheat at Čimženica again; it won't turn out well there, believe me, in no summer has it turned out well there...! Well, if you still have any of my share, give it to Izidor so that he might think of old Lukež now and then!"

He was somewhat touched when he noticed how the tears flowed down my cheeks. Father's face fell because he surely expected that Lukež would will his share to him, and not to me.

The wounded man said: "You will certainly see to everything when I'm gone, Polikarp, because you were my friend and comrade. But don't go to too great of an expense! If you would, just put a wooden cross where I will have my eternal resting place. If, of course, a cross doesn't cost too much!"

He asked to be given some water. He drank, but could not drink much. He also asked to be lifted a little, and for some rags to be put under his back, because his bones were beginning to ache.

The two of us tried to satisfy his wishes. At the same time, we lifted him onto one side in order to shove something soft under him. We had to remove the point that was stuck in his chest, because his head moved and the blood began to flow from the wound. The long talk had also tired him and he began to grow confused. He raised his voice and asked: "Do you hear them, how the cannons are roaring? Victoria! Victoria!" The blood choked him and he died on the hard pallet before the chaplain came from Poljane…

When day broke, we followed the tracks that the robbers had left. A little way up we came to a place still covered with blood. There they had slaughtered the two sheep stolen from us.

A few steps farther a human corpse lay in a pit by the path. It was the gypsy Dušan, who had been shot. We buried him right there without any pity, like a dog who died outside his fence.

We did everything as befitted the events after Lukež died. We buried him near the church wall in the ceme-tery of St. Martin's at Poljane. We put a wooden cross at his head.

In Lukež's trunk I found a paper with the image of St. Luke the Evangelist. I nailed this image onto the cross, but the rain soon washed it off…

Lukež had only been in the ground at St. Martin's two days when death again visited Visoko. And that death was most terribly connected to my own person. As long as I lived, it knocked on my door with its bony fingers. But I learned how just are the ways of divine providence, and how pure is the truth that the Creator visits sinners even by visiting their children, and from generation to generation.

One evening when all had become dark and we were sitting at our meal, old Pasaverica burst into the house and sat down on the bench by the door, saying: "I don't ask for supper, Visokan, I ask only for shelter, because I am exhausted and so terribly weak."

Before us was an old woman who looked as if she had just left the funeral bier. We took pity on her and, because father did not answer, the servant girl prepared a humble place for her on the bench by the stove. We offered her what was left of the supper, but she did not want to, or could not, eat.

When we had prayed she asked the family to leave, and for father and I to stay with her for a short time. She said that she had something important to tell us, and she hoped that I knew how to write, and that it was her intention that some of her words should be written down.

When the family had left, old Pasaverica spoke approximately thus: "I have wandered much about the world and today I fear that I am to die far from home. All the days I carried goods heavier than those your horses carry, Polikarp. And what I earned at this was lighter than a chicken feather! But Agata and I had to live and so I dragged on as long as I could. Today I have wearied and the earth calls for me. And why not, when I am eighty years old and have been oftener hungry than full during those eighty years!"

Father gruffly demanded that she say what was to be written. He wanted to go to bed and did not enjoy wasting overly much time with a beggar woman.

"Oh, Polikarp, don't think ill of a person who will soon come before the Judge who will one day judge you, too, should she try to lighten her poor soul with talk and so drive away the fear of death, which is, after all, the worst thing that can come over us!"

I prepared everything in order to write. "What shall I write?" I asked.

"Write," she sighed, "that first of all I greet the little, abandoned orphan, dearest Agata, write that I greet her over the hills and valleys and that I thought of her at my death! God is my witness that at this moment I think more of her than of myself! I am dying in a foreign land, and yet the worst thing is that I will no longer see little Agata, to whom I was grandmother and mother in one…! Yes, write all of that so that the little girl can read it, and you mustn't think that she is not schooled in reading and writing."

I wrote all of that down slowly and faithfully. Then she continued: "I have done well on this journey! For months I have dragged about the mountains, but people do not care to buy. And it is even harder to buy something from them if you do not want to pay a price that will certainly ruin you… Here are fifteen pieces of linen. Oblak has everything and it has all been paid for, too. When he goes to Passau to trade, let him take care that he gets a good price for my pieces because they are truly beautiful. Neither will he want for Jesus's blessing if he sells high and so takes care of the orphan who will from now on be abandoned in the world like a leaf that has fallen into the water."

She cried, and my heart was also breaking. But father remained morose and rose sleepily.

"It will be best," continued Pasaverica, "if Oblak himself buys them, because I know that he would not want to shortchange a poor widow…There are ten Venetian gold pieces sewn into my clothes. Use these and what Oblak will pay, Polikarp! When you take the bishop's wine to the German lands, take all of this with you and deliver it to my Agata! I have trust in you, Visokan, because I know that in your long life you have never stolen anything from anyone!"

I do not know how it happened that she spoke these last words somehow more loudly, but they visibly effected father, because he scratched his gray hair in aggravation. Displeased, he retorted:

"What the devil has driven you about the world? You should have stayed in your homeland, which is richer than ours and where people live better!"

"Polikarp!" she sobbed, "what do you know about how we lived in Germany? Who would trudge like all over the world like a stupid mule if he could live at home and watch the green river beneath him…! I had a good husband, a fine husband, he cared for me, he cared for his sons. They forced a strange faith on us, but we rejected it. And let your son write that old Pasaverica died true to the Catholic religion. We had a small house, we had a little field and woods. But what of it, when almost every summer the Swede came to our country and burned our roof, trampled the ears of grain, so than there was not even cooked grass to put on the table! If it was not the Swede, then the emperor's men stormed in and wanted to have the last rags from our bodies, there was not a house they did not burn, not any grain they did not trample! Happy are your women that they did not know the Swedish nor the emperor's cavalry, nor hunger, which crushed us every summertime. So it was!

It was difficult for her to speak, so she was silent for a while. It seemed to me that father was no longer sleepy, and I had the impression that he was considering something. She began again:

"We built the house up a few more times, but they burned it for us again. It was said that the Swedes, like the emperor's men, were looking for soldiers, and that they paid them well. Then my husband decided to join the army. He gave the child and me to a good neighbor for protection and then he set out. Nothing was heard of him for a long time. The neighbors whispered that he had forgotten me and the child. For such an army is merciless and many Catholic men became wild in it and went over to the Swedes and thus fought against their own faith.

She again had to rest because her breathing was difficult and the words would not come. Then she said this:

"But he was heard from! He sent me a letter in which it was written that the emperor's men had achieved a great victory at Nordlingen, that he had cut very many Protestants to pieces, and that they had also taken a great number of Swedish generals—I hope that they hung them in the pines!—and captured much baggage and other stores. My husband sent me money with the letter, so that I would no longer be a burden to our neighbors. Later on, he occasionally sent me more so that I could leave. He informed me through trustworthy people that he would bring so much back from the army that we would build and roof a new house and that we wouldn't have to live like the beasts of the forest."

Her tears flowed. When she breathed easier she continued thus:

"But there was no end to the war! It raged another ten or fourteen years, until the emperor and the queen reconciled themselves enough to talk of peace. Peace was finally agreed upon and the soldiers hurried to their villages. Some did not return because their bones rested in Saxony or God knows where. We waited for our man, but he never came. I was already losing hope that he would be no more. Then one day the shepherds brought news to our village that in a lonely place up in the forest lay the body of a murdered Swede. I cannot tell you how, for some reason, this news shook me, I did not know why. Arriving where the dead man lay, we recognized my husband! When they picked him up and turned him over, he had an ugly wound in his back, from which his life had flowed out."

My father looked timidly from under his brow and his fingers played incessantly on the table.

"So our hopes," said Pasaverica "drifted away on the water! We were left beggars and I didn't have any hope for my son. When he grew up, he married a girl with a respected name. But God still kept beating me! Sickness came and entered almost every house; in this one and that, it took all that lived. My son and his wife had to die, too. The only thing they left me was the child, who could barely move its arms and legs. The child was baptized in the name of St. Agata. And that child buried itself so deeply in my soul that I was happier for it than for my own life! But little Agata wanted just to eat and eat. She drove her grandmother into the world to collect penny after penny, to suffer only so that the innocent child would not suffer. Never ask me, Polikarp, why the devil drives me through the world and causes me to struggle among you! If you were in my place, you would do no different. You, too, would wander through the world to scrape for a piece of bread for a child if the child was all that was left after your son died!"

She was seized by anger and began to curse her husband's murderer.

"May the hand that slew my husband be cursed a hundred times! If he still lives, may his members dry up and may worms eat his living body! And if he is dead, may he lie in the most white-hot corner of hell, and may the devil's servants pull the skin from him night and day! How differently we would have lived had the hand of God crushed that murderer earlier! But now the young girl must work for strange, although respectable, people! And I am dying in a strange land and Agata is not with me! I only wish that that cursed man could see me at this moment, as I suffer and die so hard! He put an end to everything: my husband, Agata, and me! May he be cursed unto all times! He will be cursed because a dying widow curses him!"

The hairs on my head nearly stood on end at these unchristian words! When she finished cursing, father—

believe me, he was as white as the winter snow— asked, quaking somewhat:

"Where exactly are you from, Pasaverica?"

"The village," she sobbed, "is called Eyrishouen."

The Visokan got up as if struck by lightning and, from behind an icon on the wall, he drew a bunch of old papers which he had put there knowing that no one would steal such things. He spread these papers on the table and looked and looked until an old soiled paper appeared between his fingers. He must have had to read something on that small paper very carefully because his eyes bulged from beneath his forehead like two apples.

Pasaverica had eased her soul with her cursing. Peacefully and without anger, she said: "Yesterday, when I was traveling over Gaberška Mountain on the way here to Visoko, night overtook me and I could no longer reach a human settlement. I spent the night under God's stars and fell asleep very quickly. And behold, my husband appeared to me in my dreams. He was white as wax and all of the clothing on him shone. He was without life's sins, for we know well that a murderer takes on all of the sins of the one he has murdered. Thus my husband appeared to me without sin and he shone as the sun shines in the sky. Then he said to me, 'Marija, I have come for you!'"

And once more she repeated: "Marija, I have come for you!"

At this, father groaned: "Pasaverica, is that your true name?"

She replied: "That is how they call me in this country. In truth, however, my name is Schwarzkoblerica, because Jošt Schwarzkobler was my lawful husband."

83

Father answered nothing. Like a felled pine, he tumbled headlong onto the bench and from the bench onto the floor. He remained lying there and the blood filled his black face, and he groaned and groaned, just as if he had been struck and crushed by a heavy blow.

On the small paper, which was old and soiled, a clumsy hand had written: "Jobst Schwarzkobler from Eyrishouen." The letters were barely distinguishable from one another, but today the Lord God himself had probably renewed letter after letter so that each one glittered for Polikarp Khallan, as a star glitters on us from a clear sky.

That evening, however, I did not learn the full truth, and still did not know anything for sure, and not all of it.

VI.

The next morning, we found Marija Schwarz-kobler dead on the bench...

Father had already regained consciousness the previous evening. He crawled up the stairs to the upper quarters as if drunk, and climbed onto his bed in his clothes. That is how he was still lying the next morning when I came to him and told him that I must go to Loka because it was the feast of St. Ahac. He did not answer, but only winked at me to sit down on the chair by his bed.

He gazed continually at the ceiling; only now and then did he look at me. His face had changed, and his eyes had also changed. Once a cat had fallen from the Visoko roof and broken its back in such a way that it dragged the rear part of its body behind it. Father's look was just as it was when he watched that cat drag its crippled body behind itself! Perhaps he had fully realized his condition, but his crippled and broken soul was probably only half conscious in him.

He stammered: "To Loka? Then go to Loka, but a thing or two has changed! Jeremija will not like it, but it cannot be helped! Inform him that what he offers is too little! He will not like it but I cannot help him, it is too little!"

He then added this: "At Loka find Valentin the tanner! Tell him that I want to have Trubar! It will be better with me if the pure divine word flows like oil into my soul!"

He fell silent and once again stared at the ceiling.

I waited yet a little while, but when father spoke no more, I left, got on a horse, and set out towards town. There was a quite large fair there on the feast of St. Ahac. I overtook fairgoers carrying hides and baskets, panting on the way to Loka to sell what they had made.

Thoughts of father would not leave my mind, father, whom I had left at home so miserable and alone. What was it about that Jošt Scharzkobler, whose presence on this earth I had never been aware of before? But yesterday he had risen from his grave and come to Visoko! I could not doubt that something terrible, which binds the living and the dead, must have existed between him and father.

Pondering thus, I rode up to the manorhouse which we called "Schefferten," and which lies halfway on the road from Visoko to the town. The holding was not large and did not have the right to a special tithe or noble ancestry. It brought in so much less because its owners neglected it and worked it poorly. For a long time, the owner of this small estate was lord Pečaher, a well-known Carniolan countryman and rich nobleman, who often loaned money to the Loka bishops. And these lords always needed money, since they had fled from the Swedes so many times! Yet it was said that the crooked bishop's staff was a poor lord and that anyone who wished could deceive it. Lord Pečaher did not like

Schefferten and the year before he had sold it to the heirs of Skarlikij, who probably obtained more than enough money for it from the bishop of Ljubljana. But even after this sale, the manorhouse remained deserted. If you were riding by, you did not see a soul around. Only rarely did an old maid or an even older servant happen to appear in the area of the building.

Today, however, to my great surprise, a young servant was leading a saddled horse about the yard, and right nearby the trade road was standing a young woman dressed as the daughters of nobles dress in our time. She had a whip in her hand and she was surely just wanting to get into the saddle. I cannot say that she was wonderful of face and full of body, but she must have been haughty and daring. She looked at me rather scornfully—that is, in a manner in no way becoming a modest young woman. She did not lower her eyes at all when I daringly returned her gazes. Who was that woman?

At about ten I arrived at the town gate. I paid the gatekeeper the duty which the Loka elders had rights to at that time. There were still many sellers on the square and baskets stood close by one another. The town scribe was collecting the market tax and the paving tax, which all of the people were loath to pay. Some lords had also set their goods out for sale, but they did not pay the market tax, for a lord always enjoys his privileges.

I put the colt in Wohlgemuet's barn and then, when the buying and selling was just about to begin, I again went to the square to look for Valentin the tanner to tell him what father had ordered.

Just then Mihol Schwaiffstrigkh marched into the crowd carrying a large drum with him. He stopped in the middle of the square, beat his drum, and then called out that in the name of the lord baron Janez Krištof-Mändel, the town magistrate and proxy of the most merciful prince and bishop in Freising, he was proclaiming to one and all that today the lord's granary would be open and that no one could sell on the square while there was selling at the granary.

It was as if he had poked about in a wasps' nest, so enraged were the buyers and sellers. There was arguing and, most of all, demands that the market tax, which was paid in the expectation that it would be possible to sell goods, be returned. The townspeople were also angry because they preferred to buy for a lower price, well knowing that the bishop demanded a higher price for poorer grain at his granary.

The bakers and tavernkeepers stormed onto the square, and among them was the famous ruffian Bergant from Oslovska Street. Others who always joined the troublemakers came as well, even though the market-goers had little use for them. The throng made a noise like bumble bees beneath the moss.

A very old peasant had the first word. He walked from group to group and yelled: "So once again he's sat on your empty heads, Loka calves! He'll do it to you many more times because he knows you, and that you would chew sand if he were to strew it in front of your empty snouts instead of millet! You think that you're eating meat when you're gorging yourselves on burnt turnips!"

In this way, he fearlessly cudgeled the Loka inhabitants until the tavernkeeper Bergant shouted at him:

"And what would *you* do, you old fool?"

"What would I do?" the other answered. "I would issue a complaint, a complaint of the highest! And I would soon tame your bishop! Ej, Loka turnips, our estates still exist, there is still German Gradec, and the emperor too still lives, and he is, after all, something more than your bishop, who only sheers you, you sheep! Yes, you're a bunch of sheep, Loka burghers—why do I say burghers, you, Loka idiots!"

Mihol Schwaiffstrigkh, who had in the meantime drummed through the whole town, was again returning over the square and stopped before the old man who was yelling.

"Hello, Jernač Schiffrer!" he addressed him, "you're here again! Do you want to lodge another complaint, so as to put on some fat, as you did when the peasants complained about the tax! I know you well! You're a fat bird, but you stripped the fat you from the peasants, whom you rob worse than any lord, you hungry voivode!"

Immediately some of them spoke up and agreed with Mihol Schwaiffstrigkh, and the old voivode quieted down. Some woman also had to have a word, a certain Lokan who the devil had long ago rendered disagreeable and snappy. She rushed in:

"Jesus! Jesus! how he made fun of our bishop and lord! As if they had herded cows together! Mihol, tell it in the castle so they write it down! Jesus! Jesus!"

I asked Wohlgemuet, who had plunged into the crowd out of curiosity—who in Škofja Loka was not curious!—who that little peasant was that so whetted his tongue on the square. Wohlgemuet answered me that it was the voivode, Jernač Schiffrer, from Bitnje, who had in his time defended the rights of the subjects against the bishops Vid Adam and Albreht Sigismund.

"What?" raged the drummer, "he grumbled against the bishop and belittled our highest lord? Huh?" Mihol looked about angrily. "Who can say exactly what? What words did he use? Maybe he spat something else out? Who will be a witness?"

But no one wanted to speak up and even the woman who before had called on Jesus disappeared.

But the little peasant did not lose his courage. He screamed with all his might, "Just don't explode, Mihol, or it'll stink up the whole square!"

An old woman had forced her way through the throng to the screaming man and she sobbed:

"Do you always have to quarrel, Jernač, when after all you know how it is! It will again end with them dragging you to the castle, and how long has it been since you sat out the last six weeks up there? The wheat will have to be sown, the litter will have to be fixed, and will I have to see to all of that myself if they drag you to the castle jail? You have five children, all of them already grown, and it is high time that you finally wake up and come to the right realization that Schiffrer won't be more power-ful than the bishop in the castle, even if he lives a thou-sand years."

"Quiet, wife," retorted Schiffrer, the combative voivode of the Loka subjects. "What you know, I know just as well! Only I don't want the rotten castle lords to think I'm afraid of them! I'm not afraid of them at all and I wouldn't be afraid of them even if I didn't have the chief of the estates on my side! But I have him, so you know, Mihol!"

At those words Schiffrer went off with his wife because the Loka pavement was nonetheless getting too hot for him, especially when he noticed that Lord Blaž Triller was coming. The latter was at the time the first lord in the city after the town judge and the castle scribe, because he was the keeper of the castle granary. That was a good and important position which nicely maintained anyone who had it. It had also enriched Blaž's quite expansive belly, which rested with great difficulty on two short legs, as is often seen in Loka with well-fed burghers.

The lord garneter puffed over the square and called to the crowd:

"Obedience, people, obedience! What will become of us if we do not show obedience to the power that is given us by God? The granary is unlocked, the granary is full, there is no grain in the world like that I have in the granary! The granary is unlocked and will be selling until three. Then you too will sell on the square and no one will bother you."

"Who will buy anything more then," someone remarked angrily, "if you first force the 'new' grain from the tithe on everyone?"

"My good friend," the garneter sweetly refuted him, "if you don't like the Loka market, the town wall is so built that you can pass through the town gate to where you came from! How are our lord bishops, how are we who are their servants to live if the granary doesn't bring in at least something?! Do you think that the bishop doesn't have any payments to make? And who pays for the assessments, ordinary and special, since there is never an end to these devilish wars? What do you pay? But the bishop pays until he is blue! So what are you complaining about? So, the granary is open; whoever wants good grain can come to the storehouse! That's it! There won't be any selling on the square! That's it!"

And, indeed, the subjects and burghers had to give in. Only the baker Feguš, who formed the holy hosts and sold them to the pastors in both valleys, agreed: "It's true, the lords must live too!" It was easy for him to speak: if grain became expensive, he raised the price of his wafers, and by more than the increase in grain.

I found Valentin in his small room at the tanner's. The holy scriptures lay before him, for there is no other such large and fat book in the world. He received me uncordially, as was his habit. I told him that father had fallen seriously ill at Visoko, that he was calling Trubar, and whether he knew where Trubar was to be found.

A fire shone on his dead face and he answered: "Go and take care of your errands if you have any in town! Trubar will come! Polikarp is dying because a man must die, though he knows not the day nor the hour. The whole time that Adam lived was nine hundred thirty years, and he died! Enos lived nine hundred fifty years, and he died! Now it is Polikarp's turn, and I fear that his soul is weighed down with baggage, but he calls for God's word and the true servants of the word. Trubar will come!"

When I returned to the upper town, most of the sellers had already left. Only the most thick-headed and poorest were screaming for their tax back. The demand remained unfulfilled, because those who were dissatisfied were told that they could sell when the storehouse closed.

Jeremija Wulffing and his daughter were waiting for me at Wohlgemuet's tavern. His two sons were sitting at the table as well. The father was showing great satisfaction, but the sons were not at all in a good mood.

Margareta hurried up to me and handed me a little paper on which—as I had asked her—she had written down the song that grandmother was singing that evening. The brothers immediately called out that she come back to the table and not offer herself, because it was a day for buying grain, not women.

The elder's face dropped when he saw my father, who would have to be there if anything needed to be recorded or signed, was not there.

"But where did Polikarp stop?" he asked sharply. He probably thought that father was still at the market, and that he would come after me at any moment.

I sat down at the table and answered, "He won't be coming!" "He won't be coming?" father and sons asked with surprise.

I continued: "He is lying sick in bed, and there's something else." The elder caught his breath. And the sons clenched their fists.

Acquaintances at neighboring tables craned their necks and poked up their ears, so as not to miss a word.

"What is that other thing?" Jeremija wondered. In doing so he looked up at the ceiling, just as if he was going to grab for the switch that was behind his icons at home.

Margareta was pale and sensed that the affair would not end well. A betrothal is easy to agree upon, but to undo it, especially if it was made in such an important house as was the house of Jeremija Wulffing, was difficult!

I spoke up once again: "Unexpected things have come up and father is about to die! Father says that you offer too little and that nothing will come of the agreement, even if you were to offer more. God has entered into this and father has changed his mind!"

I know well that Jeremija Wulffing would rather have suffered a blow to the face in front of the whole company gathered around him knowing that he was marrying his daughter, than be forced to listen to the words of my message. For him, a haughty and well-to-do German farmer, that message was a burning disgrace. Even before he could reply his sons' anger boiled over:

"What a disgrace! We won't swallow it!" And they were already, as was their habit, banging the table.

Like a scared rabbit coming out of the turnips, I moved from the table and looked for a way to save my body from the dangerous company. The entire tavern joined the Wulffings, hollering at me.

I carried my fearful steps onto the square in front of the beer hall, where Marks and Othinrih caught up with me. They swore, then the blows rained upon me like hail, so that I could feel the lumps growing on my rear and elsewhere. I defended myself a little but I didn't yell, as the two of them were yelling enough.

While we were fighting, a small fellow suddenly stopped by and beat the pavement with a tiny Spanish stick.

"They're fighting here. Guards!—where are the guards? Jesus and Mary! They're fighting right in front of my nose!"

I noticed that he straightened his three-cornered hat so that it wouldn't fall off of his head. And I also noticed that he had a slender neck banded with white cloth, and on his chest a large bunch of embroidery peppered with tobacco, with which he filled his pointy nose. He was Baron Mändl, the castle magistrate at the time, and I can attest that all Loka feared him.

The previous magistrate, whose name no one could pronounce,* was troublesome; but Baron Mändl or, as he was also called, Baron Flekte, even more so. In his arrogance he demanded that the castle servants greet him by bending a knee before him while putting a hand to their breasts, so paying him the homage that is due only to God in church. If one didn't demonstrate the required homage, the castle magistrate began yelling: "Flecte! Flecte!", which is supposed to mean in Latin the same as our Kneel! Kneel! That is why people said that he was "Magistrate Flekte."

No sooner did the two Wulffing boys catch sight of him than they were on their knees on the ground, hands on their breasts.

Mändl asked them who they were. They humbly answered that they were Germans, the sons of Jeremija

---

* Franc Matija pl. Lampfriezhaimbzu Pürcha

Wulffing from Davča. The answer satisfied him: "Germans? Good! You were attacked! I don't doubt it, because I know that my Germans don't fight!"

He turned to me: "You're not a German?"

Forcefully and without fear I answered, "I'm not!"

The answer shook him. "Flecte!" he yelled hoarsely, If, however, they were to have cut off my head at that moment, I would not have knelt, so strongly had the Poljane blood welled up within me! And perhaps if the bishop himself were to have stood before me, I would not have been ready to kneel, and in no way before his steward, who lived off of tithes and villeinages, which he took from us if he wanted to live.

The two attackers had knocked the hat off my head; so I stood bareheaded before the steward, and he could observe the obstinacy present in every feature of my face.

He again roared, "Flecte!" But I did not budge from my place, at which he screamed, "I'll cool your blood for you, you dog, you!"

A large crowd gathered around me. The Loka judge also came puffing, and the castle magistrate turned to him, saying: "Two hours in the stocks!"

But my obstinacy grew and I thought to myself: I won't kneel! Do what you please, old man, 'til you've had enough.

The town beadle had already seized me and was dragging me to the place on the square where a group of three stakes, none of which were yet occupied that day, had been driven into the ground.

There Mihol Schwaiffstrigkh was waiting, and he had three blocks with him, one for each stake.

Without objection I laid down, and Mihol bound me to the stake with great dexterity and put my legs in the block and locked it with a key so that I could not budge from that shameful place.

Schwaiffstrigkh said to me: "You've fallen into my hands sooner than I expected! Ej, ej, but it's usually like that, it begins with the stocks and ends with Gavžnik!— Now someone will surely give me something for wine!" He went off in the direction of Wohlgemuet's tavern.

Someone brought my hat and threw it down in front of me, but not close enough so as that I would be able to reach it.

The sun burned and soon I was suffering from the heat and thirst.

I was so ashamed that I did not dare look around. The people who had gathered dispersed in a little while, and another torment began. In the houses on the upper and lower sides of the square, faces appeared, mostly women's, and calls were taken up from window to window across the square:

"Whose is he?" "Did you see, did he steal something?" "He's from Visoko!" "He won't come to any good if they've got him in the stocks!"

So those questions rained down upon me, while I was feeling myself innocent, unjustly stuck in the stocks!

When the faces disappeared from the windows and when no one cared about me any longer, I felt sorry for myself. After all, I had been attacked, but they punished me, probably because I was not German! But for no money would I have been ready to shed a tear; and in truth not a drop ran from my eyelashes. The Lokans were not able to enjoy a Poljane man sobbing!

A bit after that, wild anger and extreme passion were once again shaking me. If the castle magistrate had been in my power and a weapon in my hand, that man's life would have been in very great danger! I ground my teeth, but a curse would not come to my tongue, because even in those bitter moments I was aware that the faith to which I wanted to remain true unto death does not allow a man to curse, even if he be in the stocks. My holy patron then inspired me with the thought that the stocks were a part of that repentance that I had to do for my father—the heathen!

Sweat and thirst tortured me, for the sun was still burning. Like the Savior on the Cross I stammered a few times that I was thirsty. Not a single soul paid attention to my stammering!

But my suffering had not yet reached its peak, even then. I still had to endure the final drop.

Our pastor, Fr. Janez Kašper, passed by. The one who had come to Poljane after Fr. Karel Ignacij, and whose surname was Jager. He was surprised and halted at the site of my disgrace. He looked me over a few moments. I would have preferred to disappear into the ground, instead of having my spiritual shepherd looking at me.

"Well just look, you're Izidor! And in the stocks! It was a bad moment for me when I paid the debt today on the loan that was made for the parish with the parish dean, and when I had to pay very high interest because the parishioners collect money so slowly! But this moment is worse, Izidor! I was very mistaken about you!"

He shook his head and set off for Wohlgemuet's tavern, where he kept his small horse.

After that most bitter blow there was yet some comfort.

Margareta Wulffing came up to me, all tearful and pale. She brought me a dipper of water mixed with wine for me to quench my thirst. Then she wiped my face and wet hair with her apron, and a pleasant, new sense of strength washed over me.

The girl spoke not a word, but I hoped that in her heart she held no hatred for me, who was obedient to his father's words, which every child must bow to!

When the two hours of my suffering had passed, Mihol unlocked the stocks and let me go with some jesting remarks.

I hurried to the shed, saddled the horse myself, and led it off so quietly that the Wohlgemuets did not notice me.

And I kept the horse close to me through the town and hid my shamed head behind its mane. The traders' servants, standing with their donkeys in Oslovska Street, nonetheless spotted me. They burst out in laughter and guffawing. Only outside of the town did I crawl into the saddle and ride off, sadly, in the direction of my father's house.

When almost at Visoko I came upon Tanner Valentin, who was quite diligently marching along the trade road, small bundle in hand.

He turned onto the footbridge and waited in front of the house for me to ride up. He asked where father lay. Thinking that he would have something to tell father about Trubar, I led him upstairs.

In the passage he unwrapped his bundle and deftly got into a frayed black robe, and, in a brief moment, had changed into another man.

He went in to father. He stopped at the door, raised his hand, and solemnly declared: "Polikarp! Valentin, grandson of Felicijan Trubar, blesses you in the name of the Father, the Son, and the Holy Ghost!"

Father motioned to me that I should leave the room. I stayed in the hall, but the words coming from father's bed could not be heard clearly. Yet Felicijan Trubar's grandson, who was, as I now knew, a chaplain of the Lutheran faith—formerly I think they were called "predicants"—spoke a great deal and loudly. Father's groaning was mixed in with his words of comfort, which I could also not understand. At times the predicant also sang something and then once more gave praise, but I could not make out the words. Frequently they seemed to be whispering to each other because then their voices, which could have reached me from the room, grew quiet.

I must say that my heart was rent while I was crouching there outside, without the courage to do something, while the Lutheran labored to eternally confine my father's soul to hell.

Someone rode into to the Visoko yard. He tied his horse to the walnut tree that stood there, then came up the stairs with a heavy tread.

The tall, broad figure of our pastor Janez Kašper appeared in the upper hall. He said kindly: "On the road, and even before, I was told that your father Polikarp had taken ill. So I have come to visit him in his sickness, as is my duty."

Without hesitation, he headed for the room in which the sick man lay. He did not wait for my answer. However, the fear of such an unexpected visit had so overwhelmed me that I could not have answered even if I had wanted to.

With the words, "A couple of words of comfort will do him good," the pastor opened the door and entered. I, too, entered with him.

But our spiritual shepherd immediately halted, as if he had been turned to stone. The predicant Valentin, Felicijan's grandson, stood by the sick man in a black robe, with a white linen cloth around his neck. He had just extended his hands, exactly as our priests extend them to give a blessing.

Since it was still quite light in the room, he recognized the pastor, Janez Kašper. He immediately stopped the blessing and jumped from the bed. A chalice and plate, which are used in the Lutheran service, appeared on the small table.

It was completely obvious to pastor Jager that there was a service being held, and that it was not a Catholic one. And it became even clearer to him when Valentin Trubar began waving his hands at him and yelling:

"Slave of Beelzebub, why do you stand on the path of God's servants? Here at the clear spring of the pure gospel a pasture of the true word of God has been created. I am on guard here so that you don't lie on the green grass; lie in the mud of your Babylonian filth! Now get out of here, you were not called!"

The Poljane pastor did not condescend to quarrel with the predicant. He turned away in silence. I downheartedly left the room with him.

In the hall father thought, because he did not know what words to speak. He must have been very overcome at the thought that, at that time in his own parish and despite his labor for the pure faith, a Lutheran predicant could spread his heretical confusion, which was thought to have been completely driven from the land by bishop Chroen. Bitter feelings filled the heart of our spiritual shepherd and he had a right to be angry when behind his back a devilish seed was being sewn in the field he tended. With true sadness, he said:

"It hurts right inside when I see the heretic placing the soul of the old sinner in the stocks. God forgive me, Izidor, that I speak this way about your father! But those stocks are more shameful than the ones on the Loka square in which I just saw you! Believe me, it is so! The new rectory gives me so much trouble, the parishioners don't collect money, and they also simply neglect confession and holy communion. And now this, and in a house that is the richest in the community! I was blind but today my eyes were opened! Immediately today, I am writing a letter to Ljubljana so the bishopric can take whatever steps it deems necessary."

I fell to my knees before father, begging that he would not heap such shame on our honorable name and that he have mercy on the innocent beneath our roof who were faithful to the Catholic Church. He would not be swayed. I lamented before him and shed tears like a child.

At the walnut tree, I untied the horse and led it after father because I did not want him to get in the saddle in front of the house and thus escape my pleas. I accompanied him to where the Sora splits and where it is shallow enough for us to carry things and ride through the water.

The whole time I beseeched him to forget his report. I battled with father Janez Kašper as Lord Jesus battled with his bitterness on the Mount of Olives! I also—which was perhaps a shameless audacity—refused to release the horse to him until he had heard my plea.

At long last, he relented and we agreed that I would pay twenty German gold pieces for a new statue of St. Stephen for the right side of the altar in the church of St. Martin at Poljane, which the pastor had ordered from master Remp and which he would have had to pay for in installments. Only then did I help him into the saddle.

A week later I paid twenty German gold pieces at Master Remp's. He handed me a receipt, which the town scribe had prepared, and was happy to have gotten the money so quickly.

I gave the receipt to father Janez Kašper, who promised me that the next Sunday he would mention that the Visoko house had paid for St. Stephen to the parishioners.

Father Jager thus did not report us to the bishopric, but neither did he make mention from the pulpit of that which he had promised. The predicant had angered him terribly and he could not forget all he had experienced at Visoko.

When I went into the room to father, Valentin Trubar had not yet left. In the meantime, father had gotten up and called me to help him.

With great difficulty we hauled the iron chest out of the chaff sack. Father unlocked it and took out ten golden coins and handed them to the predicant, saying, "It is right that he who serves at the altar should live from it!"

Never was I so sorry about money leaving the house as I was on that evening!

Valentin Trubar took the ducats and disappeared into the night.

We put the chest back in the chaff sack. And father crawled onto his bed and once again slept on his money night after night.

I saw a good deal of evil that unhappy day!

VII.

The next morning father was calmer. His speech attested to the fact that something had quieted his inner turbulence. When I went in to him, he ordered me to sit down, and I immediately knew that he wanted to tell me something which, until that time, he had not told me.

Indeed, he began speaking and he went on for a long time:

"That man from Loka consoled me. He told me that I needn't yet despair of eternity. But what I've been charged with must pass, else I won't be worthy of the mercy I need so badly. What I am about to charge you with, Izidor, carry it out if you want to help your father, who in just a little while will depart this world!"

He wanted me to swear to fulfill his will; but he demanded that I swear on the holy gospel. I was ready to swear but I wanted to swear only by God and Mary, the Mother of God. I quarreled with the old man who was my father, and who was dying. Finally I relented enough to swear by God, the Mother of God, and the holy gospel!

That concession was a great sin and I have faint hope that at the Last Judgment it will be forgiven! Then father continued like this:

"I'll tell you this so that you know everything and don't have to guess at anything. You'll be ashamed of your father, but what happened happened, and Valentin Trubar instructed me to reveal everything to you. That I will have a hard death, you would notice yourself, even if I were to hide my evil life from you. Father Valentin commanded, so listen!"

"I came into the world somewhere in the Poljane Valley; you don't have to know the place. I don't know whether I had a legal father; I didn't know him. For as long as I can remember I lived with my mother, who served the lady Doroteja Suzana in the castle at Brdo. What I remember is that mother and I were in the evangelical church, for at Brdo there was a congregation of the most reverent servants of the holy gospel. They proclaimed the pure word of God to us and showed us the right path to heaven."

"When I was twelve years old, the authorities in Ljubljana ordered Lady Doroteja Suzana to leave Brdo. She took me and mother with her and settled in a German city called Nuremberg. There I became even more steadfast in the holy gospel but I am sorry that later I didn't live by it. In the twentieth year of my life, Lady Doroteja Suzana died. Soon after, my mother died as well, so that I was alone in the world. Then I roamed about and met many ne'er-do-wells. When the Swedes got into the German War and when Lord Wallenstein called the people to his colors, I joined with the emperor's army. I was still very young at the battle of Lützen, where the Swedish king and our general Count Pappenheim fell. After that I stormed about Germany and took part in truly memorable battles."

"Lukež was serving in my unit too. How he came to us, where he had trailed about before, I don't know. Nor would I ever ask him about it, as he did not question me about where I had wandered before. It emerged by chance that we were kin and both from this valley. From then on, we stayed together like twins. He was better than me; he didn't drink, didn't game, and didn't care for women, which I can't say for myself."

"We lived a wild life. We were fighting for the faith, but there was no faith in either the imperial or Swedish ranks. Woe to whomever we raised our weapons against! A human life was worth no more than an apple you knock from a tree. We burned, we stole, wherever we could get something; we didn't kill the inhabitants if they didn't defend themselves; we did the women every wrong; we didn't murder children, although those from Brandenburg and Hungary committed such deeds. We lived in such a way that Lucifer must have rubbed his hands in glee, but we didn't give a thought to death! We ate and drank and threw dice until the devil took everything we had captured in the field and robbed from the villages. Yes, we lived a wild life! And that life now weighs on my neck, so I'm dying hard! Believe me, I'm dying hard!"

He rested a while, drank some water, and then went on:

"When they stabbed Lord Wallenstein, we came under Count Gallas. The captain liked to drink and didn't worry whether there were any stores. Therefore, we often suffered from hunger, so Lukež and I got sick of him and one quiet night rode off to join the Swedes. At that time, Duke Bernard, whose name came from some German city that escapes me, was in command. He was a devil in the form of a man, but I know he didn't believe in the devil, and even less in God. He took us from battle to battle; one was more wonderful than the next. We lived well. We took the last farthing from everyone, be he papist or Protestant. Truly, those were times a cavalryman likes to remember!"

"After Bernard, we transferred to Torstenson, who always knew how to catch the enemy in the right spot. But he was a cruel master, who handed you over to the provost-sergeant for the least little thing, so that the next moment you were on the ladder beneath the gallows and, before you knew it, they had taken your breath away. None of this suited neither Lukež or me. At Jenikov in Bohemia, we battered the imperial troops and laid a thousand of them down in the field. Lukež and I had the good fortune to have an imperial general fall into our clutches. Even today, I remember well that his name was Hatzfelt. For us to grant him a pardon, he had to put up one hundred heavy pieces of gold, which we divided honorably."

Father caputures a general at Jenikov in 1645

"From that time my misfortune began! I took a liking to that golden money, and avarice laid hold of me. I put the fifty golden coins I carried on a string around my neck into a leather pouch, so that they were safely hidden beneath my cuirass. It was because of this that I remember so well that the battle was near a village called Jenikov. From then on, the pouch grew heavier and heavier from looting and stealing, and many times it blistered my skin when we went against the imperial troops at a gallop."

"But Lukež and I also had our fill of Torstenson. We joined the ranks of Banier, who was also worthless. So before long we lit out from him and again hired on with the imperial troops, where there was less grueling work and better food. Before we had fought for the holy gospel, now once again for the holy Catholic cause. Not with especially good fortune. When we clashed with the Swedes, they pummeled us, and now and then we lost generals and cannon.

At this time Lukež and I were joined by a comrade who stated that his name was Jošt Schwarzkobler and that he was from Eyrishouen, somewhere near the town of Passau. He said that he was married and that he had left his wife and child in his home village, wanting to make some money in the war. He didn't drink, he didn't gamble, and he, too, certainly carried a heavy pouch beneath his cuirass. He was older than we were, all out for himself, not that frank, and didn't like to look you in the eye.

Near Dachau in Swabia we finally, once and for all, beat the Swedes. As we were driving the enemy in front of us, Lukež, Schwarzkobler and I rode into their baggage. There, we captured a war chest we had difficulty hiding from our comrades. Nevertheless, we managed to keep it safe and bury it in the ground. Just when we were about done with the work, some Swede who was lying wounded under a smashed wagon fired his pistol at us and badly wounded Lukež. You can believe me that Schwarzkobler and I immediately strangled the gunman!

A war chest is taken at Dachau in 1648

109

Several days later word arrived that the emperor and the kings had made peace, thus ending the war that had dragged on for some thirty years, and in which I myself had had a hand for almost eighteen.

It was fine by us, too, that the war had ended. The lord generals hurried to send us off, because now, with no more stealing and robbing allowed, a soldier couldn't live. We received the necessary writs, so that the authorities wouldn't detain us on our way. The cavalrymen, who were poorly paid, were given horses, and even military equipment and weapons.

Lukež was still lying in the hospital. I handed him some money and instructed him to come to Škofja Loka later, where he would learn where I could be found. And Schwarzkobler and I set out on the journey without delay. We bought a baggage horse for ourselves and loaded it down with the war chest and other junk a man couldn't bear to carry himself.

From Dachau on, acquaintances and comrades swarmed the road, hurrying homeward, some on horseback, others on foot. We would meet foreigners coming from the north and east. They hailed us in all sorts of languages; however, since we spoke neither Spanish nor French, we didn't answer. Many of them looked at the baggage horse, and we sensed ill will in those looks. Those on foot were especially bothersome, and they insisted that two men didn't need three horses, so we could give up at least one of them, or let one of the honest men afoot climb into the saddle and rest up. These remarks were accompanied by dark looks, but no one dared use force, because we had on strong cuirasses and our loaded pistols were readily at hand!

We didn't trust anyone, neither did we trust one another. Immediately when we mounted at Dachau, two devils joined us. One sat by me, the other by Jošt. Already on the first days, we were becoming withdrawn and spoke very little. If I were to look at his pensive face, I immediately sensed that a devil was whispering in Jošt's ear: 'Why should you share? You have a pistol, you have a dagger, and on every road there are plenty of lonely places; there are also enough ditches to throw a corpse into, where no one will discover it until Judgment Day!'

And if Jošt Schwarzkobler watched my pensive eyes, he, too, knew that the devil at my back wasn't silent, and that he was also filling my ears with loaded pistols, sharp daggers, lonely places, and ditches where a murdered man could be buried. We were as cunning as two weasels and ready at any moment, so as not to be caught off guard by a pistol shot or the thrust of a long, sharp dagger. At the outset we traveled, if possible, in the company of some horseman returning from the French field of battle or somewhere else. And at night we never stayed on the road; in the evening we always looked for a settlement where we could spend the night beneath a roof, so that there would be people at hand if temptation were to seduce Schwarzkobler or me into reaching for a weapon, as the devil encouraged us to do.

Thus we trailed onward from day to day. We left behind the towns called Ingolstadt and Regensburg. One day Jošt had the misfortune of having his horse fall under him and not get up again. We maintained ourselves poorly and grazed the worn out animal even more, for we were moving through country that had just been laid waste to by generals Tiren and Wrangel, two mad and insatiable wolves. Jošt took the saddle, he didn't throw it away; he threw it on the baggage horse, even though it was overloaded as it was. From then on, I was in the saddle one day and Jošt the next. However, neither of us would allow the one on horseback to lead the horse with the goods. If the rider started off, he could also take the goods with him without trouble, because all the same an animal is happy to follow another animal. Therefore, the one on foot always led the pack horse.

We were again approaching the Danube, and I think that we were also coming close to Passau. Schwarz-kobler told me that Eyrishouen was so close that a can-non ball from the town where we were staying could almost hit it. He asked if we would divide our shares here or down in the village. Without hesitation I an-swered, 'Here!' I wasn't so unwise as to allow a divvying up in a house where Schwarzkobler and his people would have me in their hands. 'Fine,' said Schwarz-kobler, 'the road splits here: to the left it goes to Ey-rishouen, and to the right towards the border. It's time we divide things up!'

We led the horse off into a thicket and tied it to a tree. There was a little grassy patch in that thicket. We threw the goods on the ground and sat down. The war chest stood between us. Schwarzkobler said: 'We are alone and two brigands could easily steal from us when we're at the best part of the dividing! A man has to be watchful!' He pulled a pistol out of his belt, loaded it and set it down next to him on the grass so it would be immediately at hand. At that moment I too prepared my pistol so it would be handy, and at the same time I also prepared my dagger so I could use it whenever I wanted.

We opened the iron chest. It was packed to the top with white and yellow money. Schwarzkobler dug his hand into the money and stirred it. 'Watch that you don't lose a couple of your fingers,' I angrily reminded him.

He answered me with a look, and I knew that he would have rather answered with his pistol. 'You think I'm a thief, like the others?'

I answered him, 'Easy, Jošt, take it easy! Since you pulled your hand out of the money, I won't say anything more about it. Let's just get going!' 'We won't bargain long,' Schwarzkobler shot back. 'Half and half, and that's it!'

I was taken aback: 'Half and half? Doesn't Lukež get anything?' 'Who knows, if he doesn't rot in the hospital!' Jošt replied.

But I said: 'Lukež's third goes with me! We're from the same land, and he'll look for me!'

'And if he dies?' roared Schwarzkobler. 'Sure you'll take care of his third! We won't ride away like that, brother! Lukež's third will stay with me. I have a farm, you don't—Where's he going to look for you?'

'And if he dies in the hospital,' I laughed. 'You'll write for me to come, won't you? We won't ride away like that, you old devil!'

'You won't trick me!' growled Jošt. And his right hand was already inching slowly towards his loaded pistol, so that I could clearly see how his fingers moved through the blades of grass.

'You or me!' My dagger was already in my hand and I thrust it into Jošt's body below his neck from behind, so that he was covered by a jet of blood. It wet his back and also flowed over his rusty cuirass in front.

For just a moment he kept sitting and watching me in a strangely dumb way, but then he fell on his back and lay still. He moved his lips and his last words, in stuttering moans, were: 'I'll come for you!' Then he died.

I wasn't in the least terrified by the terrible utterance. 'You'll come for me?' I joked. 'If not before, at least on Judgment Day in the afternoon!' If I hadn't killed him, he would've killed me! That's, after all, the way it is in war!

I set about the work with great deliberateness and calm. I took the cuirass off him and grabbed his purse, which he carried around his neck. I was also suspicious that he hadn't wanted to part with his old saddle. I stabbed at the saddle with my dagger a few times in different places, and did indeed find some ducats for which Jošt didn't have any more room got in his purse.

I dragged the corpse further into the thicket and threw it into a ditch. I also threw the old saddle into the ditch and covered everything with dry branches that were lying about. I covered the spot where we were dividing the spoils with branches, too, and so hid the blood that had reddened the grass.

On the whole, then, I hadn't done a bad job. I loaded the little horse and, since in such wild times a man never has enough weapons, I stuck Jošt's and my pistols in my

Jošt Schwa? kob-ler'ssad death. Octobe 1648

114

belt. Not for a moment was I worried that someone would sniff me out. Who cared for such trifles in those days, when people so often came upon human corpses along the roads and let them lie until the crows and jackdaws picked them clean?

Before reaching Eyrishouen, I turned to the right in order to reach the border as soon as possible. If it were at all possible, I stayed on the trail with my two small horses night and day. I moved farther and farther, but no one was following me or hunting me like a murderer. But, I'll tell you, the nights, as I inched on through them, were empty. That infernal devil no longer sat behind me; he had disappeared, and in his place now perched Jošt Schwarzkobler. I knew that he was perched on my saddle, even without looking back at him. And I not only knew, I saw him quite well—how he sat behind me staring dumbly, a deep wound yawning on his back. Although I didn't turn my face, although I kept looking only ahead, I nonetheless saw all of that quite clearly. And he wasn't silent; he whispered to the horses' hooves without pausing: 'I'll come! I'll come for you!' So I carried him with me, even though he was lying beneath thick branches in a ditch at Eyrishouen! But then a man becomes used to such whispering too, and when I neared the border, Schwarzkobler tired and opened his dead lips less often.

I began making plans for the future. I roamed the world like a wild animal—here one day, there the next—nowhere is anything yours, nowhere a roof to sleep under, nowhere land to work! I wanted to become the owner of fields and meadows and cattle, and, in the valley where I was born, a beggar child, and where I wanted to return to, a man of worth. Meanwhile I kept a sharp eye on the baggage on horseback and joked with him, who continued to sit behind me in the saddle, though now in more of a haze. I said: 'Scream as much as you like, you won't come for me anyway, because you can't move from your place!'

I came to Škofja Loka. Everyone ran up when an imperial or Swedish cuirassier, whom they didn't often see, would approach the town in his rusty armor through the Water Gate. I stopped at the best tavern, which was even then the property of Wohlgemuet. They gave me a shed for my horses and even a special room, where I settled with my treasure. At the beginning I visited the beer halls and told all sorts of tales about my military service, usually made up, to the Loka burghers. So as not to raise suspicion, I paid my bills at Wohlgemuet's slowly; and sold my lies in the beer halls, and was glad to drink if others were paying.

Thus, in a short time, I was well acquainted with the whole town. Everyone thought I had nothing, and the town judge was beginning to worry that I would become a burden on the commune. Those were bad times to have money, but my treasure was quite safe, because no one expected me to have one!

Even the Loka bishop at the time, Vid Adam, lived in constant need. The castle magistrate, the castle gardener, and even the bishop's huntsman—everyone who served the lord's estate—sniffed about from Loka to Vipava in search of a man to lend the lord bishop something. It so happened that it was the talk of the town in those days that Vid Adam was looking for two thousand German gold pieces, and that he would put up two nice holdings at Visoko for them. Then the sun began to shine on me! I lent the lord magistrate the two thousand. When two years went by and the bishop couldn't pay, he sold me both holdings. I added five hundred of our own gold pieces, and with that the tithe was paid up and only a small villeinage, which I took care of with the wine trading, was left. So I became a landowner at Visoko, and in the eyes of the people one of the foremost men in the Poljane Valley.

To be one's own man is a great good fortune! I already desired that fortune when riding off into battle, whether it was under Gallas or under Torstenson!

I married. Vovk Wulffing from Suha had a young girl. I won the maiden, and some dowry along with her besides. She was your mother Barbara. Her older brother is even now the master at Suha, the younger Jeremija bought land at Davča, as you already know. It pleased God or, perhaps, the devil: my farm grew beautifully, the barns were filling, and my affairs multiplied!

One day a ragged man came to the house, and you could tell by looking at him that he had wandered about in the world. It was my comrade Lukež. He stayed with me, although he never asked if he could stay. He never asked about the war booty, how it was divided, and where his share was. Neither did he ask how much he would earn a year. He was my good and honored servant. I lied to him that Jošt Schwarzkobler had tricked him out of his share. He believed me, or at least he pretended to believe me. He was as devoted to me as a pup that licks his master's hand is devoted. Happy is he, later he died easily!

When my wealth was increasing, when each day I had to look at Lukež's humble face, and realize each day that Lukež knew that Schwarzkobler and I had ridden from Dachau together, I began to worry that maybe he'd done some asking about Schwarzkobler, or maybe checked around in his village and discovered that he'd been murdered and robbed. To this worry was added one that my wealth, which I had gained by another's life, would again disappear, and that my two children would become beggars and vagabonds, like their father had been in his time.

These two worries weighed heavily on me, and someone else besides added to them, who wouldn't stay put in his grave: Jošt Schwarzkobler once again began to visit me! When I caught sight of some Loka beadle coming into the valley on his errands, I right away held my breath, wondering if he was hunting me. Jošt Schwarzkobler was speaking out, and louder and louder, from year to year. He was there in my dreams at night and, if I was in the saddle, that infernal dead man again perched behind me! *I'll come for you! I'll come for you!* rang in my ears again and again, and often I writhed like a snake in my dark cellar because of the tortures! I told you all of this because that is what Valentin, Felicijan's grandson commanded.

You know how Marija Schwarzkobler died in my house and how she commended her husband's murderer to the devil. That's how hell's torment must start, as I felt on that evening!"

The old man moaned and groaned. But he regained his strength: "Listen well to me, boy, and fix each of my words in your soul! It's my wish that you become master of Visoko after me. And I'll draw up my will so that it will stand up everywhere, even at the Loka castle. I won't overly burden you, so that you, and also your child, will be able to keep the estate, for that was the intention of his grandfather in murdering and stealing all over the world!"

He uttered these words with difficulty. When he had rested a little, he continued: "As soon as you've taken care of everything after my death, set everything in the house in order, because you'll have to go on a journey from which you'll return in two or three months. Don't forget the widow and her account with Oblak of Žiri! Then saddle both pack horses; take a servant and a weapon with you, for I know that even today there are more evil people than just ones in the world. You'll ride far into foreign lands, until you come to a great river on which stands the German city Passau. The village of Eyrishouen must be near that city. In the village ask for Jošt Schwarzkobler and everyone he left behind. Find out who the strangers are that Schwarzkobler's widow spoke about, with whom his granddaughter Agata lives. Whatever it costs you, you must bring that little girl to Visoko. She'll go with you, especially since she will want to visit the grave of her grandmother. When you've brought her to Visoko, keep in mind every day that Agata Schwarzkobler is the owner of a fair half of both of your Visoko holdings; that half was paid for with Jošt Schwarzkobler's money—that is, with the girl's money. It would be my wish that you become engaged to the maiden, and that she become your lawful wife, because all the same Visoko won't be able to get long without a lady. But don't force her into this! If she would choose another for herself, pay her for half of our two holdings, so that the harm will be recompensed and all of this will be in my favor when God judges me—a murderer. You've given me your oath to do all of this, and may your tongue rot if you ever break it!"

With those terrible words, father dismissed me. It was morning on the feast-day of St. Korbinijan, which we celebrate at the end of the month of November.

For some time afterwards father continued to get up and move around. Now and then I also heard him open the iron chest and jingle the money as he counted it with his strong fingers.

Father makes his will around Christmas 1690 Around Christmas I had to go for the castle scribe, who ordered me to call for Jakob Debelak, the first sexton at St. Volnik's, and Janez Klemenčič, the second sexton at the same place. Father made his last will and the castle scribe wrote it down. And it is an old truth: Whoever makes his will is soon to die! So we knew that the hours of Polikarp Khallan, or Khallain's life, were numbered. Soon after the New Year, God's hand touched him and made him lame on the right side of his body so that he could not get up anymore, and we moved him like a piece of dead wood.

At that time I was once again sent for by brother Valentin. Again the latter spoke to Khallain a long while, and also sang and read to him from a thick book. When the singing and reading was about over, Valentin called me into the room.

God will forgive me and the Virgin Mary will pray for me that that sin may not remain on my soul! In my presence the Lutheran chaplain blessed the bread in his heretical way, and also blessed the wine in his chalice. Then he shared the bread and wine with the sick man, whom I raised up so he could partake of what Felicijan's grandson falsely called the body and blood of our Lord and Savior. When father was once again lying in his bed, he took my right hand with his left, which he could still move, saying:

I assist at Lutheran communion

"Izidor! Bless you for all of the love that you have shown me!"

I paid brother Valentin ten ducats, and then ran out of the room and into the dark attic, where I sobbed as once had the holy apostle, when he had betrayed his Teacher…

Felicijan's grandson left the heavy book with father for him to read from when death's grip would set in. The book had the following title:

The Bible, Herein is all of the Holy Scripture, the Old and New Testaments, Interpreted in Slovene, Essayed by IuriiDalmatin

And, indeed, the lord of Visoko began to slip into death's grip! His speech was labored and became a great burden to himself. As for me, may all of the saints bear witness that I also showed him the love that a son must give his father, even when he is most forsaken. Not for a moment did I tire at his bedside. His death was agonizing, terrible, and dreadful! I have not seen a man die like that.

I have seen them die in battles when the field echoed with the despairing cries of despairing sinners; but I did not notice so much fear before death, even when the provost-sergeant led his prisoners to the gallows!

Jošt comes to father's death bed Those were terrible nights. The exhausted body was refused sleep. The old man began to say that he heard different voices: now a river roared, then bells were heard in the distance. But a voice cut through the roar and intòning, and the ill man in the grip of death hated to hear it most of all—the voice of the murdered Schwarzkobler; "I will come for you! I will come for you!"

He stammered: "Do you see him? He's standing there in the dark, I can make out his face well and there is also a wound in his back with that damned dagger in it! Izidor, help!"

At such moments I reached for Jurij Dalmatin's book. I opened it at random. And it opened to the place where was written:

Have mercy on me, O God, according to they loving kindness: according unto the multitude of they tender mercies blot out my transgressions. Wash me thoroughly from mine iniquity, and cleanseme from my sin. For I acknowledge my transgressions: and my sin is every before me....

Make me to hear joy and gladness; that the bones which thou hast broken may rejoice.

Hide they face from my sins, and blot out all mine iniquities.
My father Polikarp Khallan's sad death in 1691 *Deliver me from my bloodguiltiness, O God, thou God of my salvation: and my tongue shall sing aloud of thy righteousness.*

I read this to him once or twice, until he calmed down.

He died on Ash Wednesday. At that time I renewed the promise that all the days of my life I would do penance for him who had been a great sinner, but who was also my father.

We buried him the day after Ash Wednesday. No matter how much I pleaded with him, our spiritual father, pastor Janez Kašpar, would not be moved and would not hear of allowing us to bury him at the church of St. Martin at Poljane. His words were: "Bury him in the Lutheran cemetery the Protestants once had in the Poljane Valley!"

That cemetery lay in a deserted place, and those of us living at the time no longer knew that human corpses were once buried there. It was a bit of unworked land in a corner where the trade road turns toward the village of Poljane.[*]

The most that the pastor would allow was for the neighbors to bear the dead man to that place. Catholics who had no relation to the Visoko house were forbidden to take part. Yet many of them came in spite of the stricture!

The funeral was at an odd hour. Two servants dug a grave in the morning, and at two in the afternoon we came with the body and buried it without prayers. God's mercy! May I never live through such a day again!

I observed the old customs. Since the funeral was during Lent, I "dropped the fast" for the dead man, as we say. I fed everyone that had come to the grave, just as the cotters do at their Catholic funerals. They ate, drank, and were in very good spirits. He, however, slept beneath the sod! And the more that was consumed and drunk, the more excellent the funeral became!

---

[*] The present "Ajdovskibritof" at the Videm corner.

Even at the last opportunity I did my father full honors, and, as an exception to the fast, the Visoko farm held a remembrance for the deceased on the seventh day such as had not been seen at the Poljane Catholic cemetery ever before or after. The mourners consumed a whole calf and a whole pig in addition to thirty loaves of white bread. And people drank as much wine as they desired. When darkness fell on the land the company of mourners left, merry and happy as larks!

The pastor did not like any of this, but I defended myself by saying that the master of Visoko could not have been buried otherwise if shame were not to come upon his house.

When the mourners had left and one could barely see because of the darkness, someone came up the trade road. The tall dark figure stopped by the grave and spoke while blessing the dead man below the ground with its hand. The hair of a man who happened by at the time stood on end. When he made it to Poljane he told how the deceased one from Visoko had to leave hell already on the first night and that he was hopping on his grave from the pain and waving his hands as if something were really burning him.

Thus the blessing of Felicijan's grandson became a curse for us! Since then it is said that the old Visokan haunts his grave. But God had mercy on us and commanded the rock to break away from the rim of the slope and come to rest below, right on the ground where the bones of my father, the last Lutheran in that valley, lay!

VIII.

Spring was coming and it reminded me of my father's orders.

I took care of everything at the castle, and the authorities recognized me as the owner and lord of the two Visoko farms. I had to pay whole sacks of money: I paid the registration tax, the death tax, the weekly farthings, the tenth and twentieth farthings, and God knows what else; they didn't tax me on only the air I breathed! For it is true that people lived more cheaply in the old days than today, when even my chief bailiff raises his annual wage of ten German gold pieces by two whole gold pieces; and besides I had to promise him a pair of broadcloth breeches inthe bargain, which is no trifle! These days are hard for a lord!

I was informed of what was written in the will. And it was first written that I not set aside the promises made at my father's death bed.

My brother received fifteen hundred gold pieces of our money and was to have all his needs provided for as long as he worked at home. The one good fortune was that I still had the Swedish war chest in the house. It pulled me out of the water, for otherwise I would surely have drowned.

On St. Florijan's day after mealtime, I spoke with my brother and told him that I must fulfill father's will and therefore set out on a long journey to the German lands. I encouraged him to be sensible in running the farm and not to go off on frivolous paths, as I had at times noticed before then; but most of all that he obey our neighbor, who would watch over the Visoko farm in my absence.

On St. Florijan's Day I set off for the German lands 1691

The neighbor was Jakob Debelak, a well-respected man and very experienced farmer. He had a holding next to ours and everyone deservedly respected him because for a good many years running he had been the sexton at St. Volnik's.

When the lord magistrate of the castle would come to review and approve the church accounts, Jakob Debelak was always called as well; and our spiritual father would invite him to lunch in the Poljane rectory, which meant that he sat at the same table as such a high lord as is the lord magistrate of the castle! The man was worthy of this honor because he was in all ways honest and just.

Neighbor Jakob very kindly took on the duties I asked him to. And I will note right here that he carried them out conscientiously until I returned from the German lands. And I should also add that my brother Jurij showed him obedience, so that the farm did not suffer any harm in my absence.

On St. Florijan's day, two strong horses stood saddled in your yard. On one horse we loaded some flour, grits, a few loaves of bread, and also various tools, for it often happens that on such trips you must now and again sleep in lonely places where you only have to eat what you cook yourself. My servant and I were armed like soldiers, so that robbers, who are wont to fall upon travelers in the forest, could not overpower us. I myself sat in the saddle while the servant led the loaded horse.

Towards evening we arrived in the town, where we were to spend the night, because it was still necessary to take care of this and that in Loka.

I stayed at Wohlgemuet's, as always. But the difference was marked! When I arrived before, not yet being a landlord, I had to put the animal in the shed myself and see that it got something to munch on. But now, when all of Loka knew that I was the master of Visoko, no sooner had I slid off of my horse in the spacious entrance than the tavernkeeper Wohlgemuet himself appeared and cried out to the kitchen: "The Visokan is here—see that you fix him something good, wife!" And he did not stop until both horses were put away and my goods gently and cautiously carried to the top floor, where a bedroom was reserved for me. Then, when I was going to go downstairs to the beer hall, to the place set aside for the peasants, Wohlgemuet objected: "Come on, come on, you go with me to the rooms for the better people! After all, why did I build a new hall?"

Indeed, when almost all Loka burned down in the year 1660, Kašper Wohlgemuet had built a stately new house, the likes of which there are few even in Ljubljana! Upstairs in a spacious hall was prepared a long, wide table, to which the Loka lords came in the evening to drink wine and that repulsive beverage that found its way to us from the German land some years ago. Not everyone was allowed to come in here; only those who meant something in Loka were allowed, which did not seem strange to us, since now and then even the lord himself joined this company. Neither was it strange to feel my heart beating as I followed the tavernkeeper that evening.

There were already several Loka lords sitting at the table. The castle notary, the castle garneter, the town scribe, the town baker, and some other, unfamiliar burghers were also there. They sat in the smoke amid very poor lighting. But I immediately noticed that the company was not in good spirits and that the lords wore sour expressions. I also knew why.

For Primož Bergant, who had a well-known, rough tavern in Oslovska Street, where the teamster servants stayed and where he also had a shed for their packhorses and donkeys, had sat down to the table. Primož was usually already drunk by evening. Then he liked to slip off to someone else's tavern, either out of curiosity or because his wife would not allow him more drink at home. He liked to force his way into more dignified company. And so, today as well, he arrived at the table in the upper hall of Wohlgemuet's beer hall. Crude and disagreeable, he butted in with the lordly company,

Seeing us, father Bergant said merrily: "Heh, Kašper, where have you been, you devil! I've been hollering a long time but you're not around! So bring a measure of the German oil. I've got a real craving for it!"

"Who called you," Kašper replied angrily, "and who hired you, so you can disturb the lords?"

"What lords?" Bergant answered scornfully. "If you want, you can get basketsful of such lords at Lebnik!

You live off of them? We drink your sour wine, as much of it as you don't drink yourself, and at a high price! So, bring some!"

At that moment Wohlgemuet was already throwing him out the door and shoving him towards the stairs. There he pushed him away, so that Primož had to catch himself on the wall.

"As you like—I can get drink anywhere for my money, and better than yours! To my eyes, you and your lords don't even measure up to what the horses and donkeys leave in the streets!"

He left in anger.

The lords were displeased and the garneter Triller spoke up: "If you let such people up here, you'll soon be sitting at this table alone!"

The castle notary, Janez Avguštin Schwinger, added: "What would have happened had the lord baron been with us today!"

The tavernkeeper reassured them that, in the future, he would be more careful, so that no one displeasing to the lords would come to the upper quarters. He added: "And here I have an acquaintance whom I'm sure you won't put out: he has a large holding, and Polikarp his father, who sometimes even drank at this table, captured a lot of money in the Swedish wars."

They received me gladly, especially the town baker, who hoped to buy grain from me cheaply. Others of them looked at me with less interest; but nowhere will they cast a wealthy man into the street if he behaves himself well. Yet the talk did not quite flow, because the drunken Bergant still stuck in their lordly craws and because my person somehow bothered them all the same, since we had not been acquainted before this.

There was talk of the town granary and how much grain was in it. As concerned the price, the baker suggested that it was too high. The conversation thus dragged on, slowly and sleepily, until we heard heavy footfalls on the stairs.

"Frueberger is coming and he'll be in bad humor, because once again he was groveling to no avail before the head of the estates, Volk Engelbreht!"—So spoke the lord notary.

The great haughtiness of Lord Frueberger, then the gold- and silversmith in Loka

Lord Frueberger, the gold- and silversmith of Škofja Loka, had the greatest fortune in the town in those days. He had been town judge many times and was not held dear by the castle lords, because he stood up for the burghers' rights. He was extremely proud of these merits, and, when Emperor Leopoldus conferred a noble rank upon him, it went to his head, and he became haughty, haughtier even than our barons.

At his entrance we all rose from the tables and the lord notary introduced me to the old lord, to which the latter paid no heed. He sat down at the table prepared for him, where no one else dared sit, and raised his wig a bit to wipe his pate, for climbing the stairs had put him in a sweat. Then he put some snuff in his nose, ordered German drink to be brought, and right off quarreled with Wohlgemuet, saying that he had poured him too little. He then drank, sighed loudly, and called out: "You came early today!"

The castle notary, with great respect, asked: "Your nobleness, I see that you have returned from Ljubljana in good health?"

"Those Turks would like to gobble up everything up themselves!" he muttered.

From this we concluded that he had again been unsuccessfully begging Volk Engelbreht to include him in the book of the Carniolan estates.

"How many there are in the estates," dissembled the baker, "who have far less merits than you!" Both had been craftsmen in their time—since he had become a nobleman, Frueberger had not so much as touched any work—so they spoke informally, but the goldsmith did not much like this.

"We're not talking about that!" he uttered coldly. "Leopoldus praised me—I don't care much whether that Volk Engelbreht does!"

But the baker did not leave off: "Just be satisfied, after all you have a son who takes care of the trade, so you can be happy!"

Lord Frueberger turned angrily and said: "Let's leave this talk! Do you have any news, lord notary?"

"Enough news!" he answered smartly and drew a thick letter from his pocket and placed it before himself on the table. "We're cutting the Turks' heads off all over Hungary, having a delightful time, and delighting our good Leopoldus too. My friend Marković wrote me a long letter from Ljubljana, and in the letter he informs me that our chief city in Hungary was in great danger, and that the Turks almost seized it again."

"It can't be!" Frueberger exclaimed.

The notary read from the letter: "There was also living a certain lieutenant, Fink von Finkenstein by name, in our fortress. He hailed from Prussia and lived with two young Turkish women, just as a Turk lives with his wives."

"Monstrous, monstrous!" fumed Frueberger.

"And this Fink von Finkenstein sold himself to the Turkish Pasha for two thousand ducats and was going to let the Turks into the town at the place where the defenses are weakest."

"Oh, you pig, you!" moaned the nobleman.

Then the notary added: "The Pasha was so glad that he jumped up and down. At that time our colonel, Pisterecki, was being held captive by the Turks and soon after he was exchanged for some Turkish general. He had heard about it all and, no sooner did he return to our fortress, than he informed his commander, Lord General Beck, about everything, and Beck immediately had the traitor Fink von Finkstein locked up. The latter admitted to it all, fell to his knees, and begged for his life, crying: 'What does your excellency care about a scoop of blood!'"

Frueberger was again angry: "What a nobleman! Thank God he was a Prussian and not one of our noblemen!"

Fink von Finken-stein is quartered 1687 The notary read: "But crying did not help him at all. A military court adjudged him guilty and that as a well-earned punishment—and an example for others' loathing—he would lose his head and have his body quartered, and each quarter would be hung out in a different street. Moreover, it was judged that his heart would be pulled out and he would be beaten about his snout with it—all of this in the name of justice." Thus it was decided in Buda on the eighth of April 1687, and then on the ninth of April all of it was carried out on the criminal to the letter.

"But we," put in the notary, "found this out only now, because a few years always pass before a remarkable thing finally reaches our miserable Loka!"

"That means nothing!" the nobleman cheered up, "as long as it becomes known! I must say besides, that such justice agrees with me. What I would've given to be able to watch them chop and cut him up as he deserved. Although it really is too bad that such wonderful news comes to us so slowly!"

"Soldiers," the notary calmed him, "don't like to inform about such betrayals, so we learn of them only years later."

"What a shame, what a shame," the noble goldsmith kept on. "People must be shown that we have justice, that there is no begging off! What will become of us if our generals don't care whether a scoop more or less of blood is spilt? And now, what do you say, Master Remp?"

Here he turned to a young man who had not yet uttered a word. He was sitting somehow alone at his spot and pensively staring ahead. Only now and then did he take a drink from his cup. I knew him well because he had painted the beautiful image of St. Mary Magdalene at the Lord's cross at St. Volnik's and the even more beautiful death of St. Stephen on the right altar in the church of St. Martin in Poljane. The parishioners liked these two paintings very much, and they were not too expensive. He went by the name of Janez Jurij Remp.

"Well, Master Remp," said Frueberger, "what do you say? Perhaps we two can make a small deal, which we haven't yet been able to do, although we've already talked about it a lot. What would you say to a little, not too expensive, picture in which Fink von Finkenstein would be seen lying on the ground with his head severed and the executioner striking his snout with his heart? Maestro, how much would you want for such a painting... let's say in miniature?"

Lord Remp answered right away: "For the severed head, the ripped out heart, and for, perhaps, a couple pails of blood... hold on, how much would you like to pay?"

"I'd surely pay something," answered the goldsmith, who was known as a miser, "but not too much. Times are hard and money is tight."

"Well, you see," joked the painter, "you're already shaking because of the money, as is your habit! Perhaps we'll do something cheaper? What would you say to a butcher shop with a butcher killing a big bull? If you would be satisfied with the bull and axe and only the butcher's hand wielding the axe, it would be quite a bit cheaper, lord member of the estates!"

The word "estates" seared the goldsmith. He took it as an offense and asked: "You probably meant that as a joke, Maestro Remp? But a joke about a man like me is completely out of place. Isn't that so, lords?" He looked at each friend in turn, and they dully assented: "Yes, yes!"

Lord Remp got up. "What do I care about your opinion, what good is there for me in your Škofja Loka? At St. Volnik's I got money for my picture and two are just now ready for Selce, and so I saved and scraped enough together to leave for Italy, where the sun always shines, or for Flanders, where the works of the heavenly masters draw me!"

He did not respect old age, nor did he give nobility the honor it deserves, but I nonetheless liked master Janez Jurij Remp on that occasion! When he left, the others joked about him like sparrows that you shooed from one bush to another. But Lord Frueberger was clearly looking for someone upon whom to take out his ill humor. He picked me out and acted as if he had only just noticed me. There was a spark in his eye when, according to the German nobles' custom, he asked: "And who's that?"

My pride was pricked, for I would not be writing the truth if I were to say that we are not proud and held in high esteem in our valley.

He repeated impatiently: "I am asking once more: Who's that?"

I remained silent and acted as if the words did not concern me. But when the old man repeated his question a third time, everything in me came to a boil and overflowed.

I answered: "Who's that? Where I come from it's said that once upon a time he came to Škofja Loka barefoot and in rags and that he was thankful for a piece of bread if he got it. Then in the end he plated chalices and monstrances and squeezed people so much that he was able to buy a noble rank from the emperor. Where I come from it's also said that old breeches can't be fixed, even with a big new patch sewn on. That's him!"

My heart went cold when I had poured out my anger at the proud old man in this way. And there came a day

I nastily insult Lord Frueberger

when I bitterly repented not having reined myself in on that occasion, as is the duty of a true Christian!

Blood rushed to Lord Frueberger's face and he began to shout with all his might: "Kašper! Kašper!" His wig slid off his head, and when he clumsily opened his snuff box the snuff spilled onto the table.

The tavernkeeper came running, and the goldsmith ordered him to call the servants to haul me, a stupid and crude farmer, from the table.

Wohlgemuet answered decisively: "I cannot do that and I won't do it! Izidor Khallan is my relative and he's my friend, your lordship!"

And he added: "Whatever he eats and drinks he pays for honestly!"

And, indeed, he left in a bad temper. The others left with him.

The garneter and the castle scribe were especially sullen. The garneter said: "Wohlgemuet, it gets less pleasant at your place every evening!"

And the goldsmith added haughtily: "There's no need for us only to come here!" to which the castle scribe said: "Indeed, there is not!"

When they had left, I remarked remorsefully: "I've done you great harm—they won't be back."

"Eh, so what," answered Wohlegemuet, "I often have my fill of these lords: their mouths are always full but their purses empty, there's usually not even a soldo in them! If you'd see my account book, you'd notice that almost all of them have been recorded—from the garneter to the town scribe. They're hungry chickens who watch every kernel. Let them go if that's what they want!"

Later, downstairs, he pulled the soiled old record out from somewhere. Page by page he showed me the debtors. Even the goldsmith's name was found on a number of pages and always a few months passed before the note: *paarpezahlt!*

"Let them go if they want," repeated the tavern-keeper, "because I have to constrain myself 'til I break just to squeeze a few librae out of those hungry lords!"

The next morning—it was the feast of St. Monica—I changed some gold for German currency. The young goldsmith Frueberger wrote me a letter recommending me to his uncle, who had a money changing business in German Passau.

At the castle the notary wrote out a document which said that I was an honest farmer and a subject of the illustrious lord bishop of Freising, that I was on a justified journey, and that I should not be hindered on that journey. Then I rode off with my servant.

When I came upon the young provost from St. Jakob's outside of the town in the place where the Capuchins from Kranj were building their monastery, I gave him ten Rhenish gold pieces for the cause of the new monastery, so the devout Capuchin fathers would say holy Masses for the good and successful completion of all I was journeying to the German lands to do.

The Capuchin fathers build a new monastery 1691

With God's help I reached Solnograd and also Passau. There I learned where Eyrishouen was and which holding had once belonged to Jošt Schwarzkobler. I learned that the girl was still serving honest and god-fearing people who, however, had a pack of children of their own, so that they would not be sad if Agata were to leave them.

The girl did not know that her grandmother had died, because the latter had been away from home for months on end many times. She cried when I informed her of her death. The death of old Pasaverica also badly shocked the family in which Agata served, especially because the girl was now on their hands and even the small help that the deceased had brought the house was now gone.

Then I told the girl that her grandmother had died in our house and that she was well acquainted with my father, who was also now dead. And when I told Agata that her grandmother and my father wished for her to come to our house, she did not hesitate at all. Nor did the family discourage her; on the contrary, it was apparent that a weight had fallen from their hearts.

I stayed in Eyrishoun a few more days in order to get the baptismal paper that testified that Agata Schwarzkobler was the lawful daughter of her father Janez and mother Neža and that she was baptized according to the dictates of the holy Catholic Church with the names of Saint Agata and Saint Ema. There was no way I wanted any gossip to spread in our valley when I returned to Visoko to the effect that the girl was not even of our faith. But this way I had a valid document in the house with which I could ward off evil tongues if they were to strew any harm at any time.

I am not going to describe how we traveled home, what we experienced, and how it went with us. It went well, and God's hand was obviously extended over us. St. Philip and Damian 1691 Surely the prayers of the Kranj Capuchins helped!

I ought only to say that we returned to the valley exactly on the feast of Saints Philip and Damian, and it was the Lord's day. My journey had therefore not lasted as long as I expected when I set out from Visoko.

Whenever we rode by houses, the girls who were sitting out in front rose as they recognized me and when they noticed that there was a young woman sitting behind me on the horse, which was not customary in our land. In the Visoko yard, too, the family gathered when I rode by, and my brother Jurij was not a little surprised when the first thing he had to do was to help a young girl onto the ground from the saddle.

Agata did not bring a lot with her: a bundle of rags—as we say—red cheeks, and good will to help with the work.

But my soul was relieved of a great burden when I finally had the young girl under my roof and the wish made by my father in his dying hour had been fulfilled! If I am not mistaken—in such matters and at such a time confusion can occur—Agata was then perhaps seventeen years old. She was like one of us, and at table she sat beside me, lest the family think that she was a foreigner and only a servant in the house.

She lived upstairs in a small room, and my brother Jurij and I gave her everything that had been left by our mother, so that she might live like a daughter who was born in our house.

Agata Schwarzkobler, may God bless your arrival beneath our Visoko roof!

IX.

Agata quickly became accustomed to her new life. She immediately undertook all manner of work; and as concerns diligence, I could hold her up as an example to the other servants. It is true that, at the beginning she was a bit melancholy and often cried for her grandmother. She exchanged her clothes and started to dress like us. Before long she was happier. At work or wherever, she would start singing songs, which we liked, even if she was singing in a foreign tongue. A year had not gone by and she was already twittering in our language, with difficulty at first, clumsily, and mixing in German words, so that we all had to laugh at her. She, too, would laugh and did not allow herself to be frustrated until she could speak exactly as we spoke.

She had a happy and meek nature. She quarreled with no one. Before long she had plenty of friends, all of the daughters of our peasants sought her acquaintance. On holiday afternoons these acquaintances would come to Visoko, so that there was a genuine fair around the old house, and the dark spirit that surrounded my father Polikarp and his old farm was felt no more.

When for the first time, with a baret on her head, she strode to Sunday Mass in the company of Jurij and myself, there was great marveling and approval at the church. It was judged that there were few girls in the valley as pretty as our Agata.

She was also devout. She liked to pray and she behaved so nicely at the divine service that the pastor, Father Jager, praised her when I spoke with him. He was devout and a sensible priest, only he died too soon. We buried him right by the church wall, at the small side gate.

Nor did the girl cause me worry in other ways, especially since she did not look at the men. Sometimes she went to a dance or to spinning, but always with my brother Jurij. The two of them were never absent for long, which was fine by me as master, because dancing and spinning are quite prone to spoil a young woman. That is why our spiritual father often spoke up against both in church.

From the time Agata was in the house, my brother Jurij changed completely. Before, there was not a dance at this or that mission that he did not rush off to. Nor did he ever have his fill of caroling. He invited four or even more horsemen from Poljane, Sestranska Village, and elsewhere, and then they would ride about the Loka area for entire weeks and sing from house to house. The boy had grown up to become handsome, and the girls did not disdain him. Now he stayed home. He would go to dances if Agata went with him, but she did not like to frequent dances. Jurij did not go caroling at all any more, and his best friends could not convince him, even though they had the most beautiful and best horses. He worked hard on the farm and cared for every little thing.

Thus I can write that we began a new life at Visoko and that it went well for us. We produced enough and paid the villeinage and tithes without difficulty, even though there were more of them than stones in the Sora.

About myself I cannot write anything of note. Agata was making my life satisfying—that is the truth. I did not give a thought to anything else. However, I cannot hide the fact that I began to be fond of everything about the girl, and more and more so. Her figure was more beautiful than the figure of any other girl; and her speech also seemed to me more sensible than that of all the other lasses, who did not avoid me, since after all it was known that sooner or later a young wife would arrive at Visoko. Nor will I conceal that I sometimes looked into Agata's young face with great delight and that I especially liked the few stray golden hairs about her ears that she could not restrain beneath her kerchind there was something else that ought to be written. Just as I would now and then rest my gaze on the maiden, so too my brother Jurij would gaze at her, and several times I noticed that Agata and my brother's eyes met, which never happened with me. It always pierced me inside and I would very much have liked to scold my brother, who, after all, should have known that the girl was not for him and that he ought to leave her in peace, as did the male servants.

That is all that I can write here about my person—that is, about the person of the Visoko master.

Anno 1693 at the castle I assumed a tithe in the Javor 1693 and Hubanj parishes. At the same time I bought the rights to dances in the entire valley. The bishop rented the right to allow dances for three years. For all three years I paid thirty ducats. In turn those who wanted to hold any dance always had to pay me one ducat. And there were plenty of quarrels, because the people insisted that the tax was only for dances at church fairs, where the dancing was in the open, and not for dances in beer halls and houses, which they said did not fall under the ducat tax. But I did not want to litigate, as there was no loss, and not much profit either.

These rentals, particularly the tithe, which the people paid in installments, created plenty of new duties for me. The payments had to be recorded so that later it could not be argued that more was paid than had been in truth. Here too Agata helped me because she wrote well, and thus here once again it was shown that she would be a clever lady of Visoko. Let God, He who is the first master of all masters, judge as he sees fit…!

On the feast of St. John the Baptist, there was a church consecration in the Sestranska Village mission. Janez Tičnik put down three ducats for the dance because he wanted to place three floors on the Čadež pasture—that is, one for Sestranska Village, another for Hotavlje, and the third for the Holy Cross mission at Srednja Village. Each mission had to dance by itself and right off there would be quarreling and fighting if someone would try to dance on another mission's floor without special permission!

The dance in Sestranska Village on St. John the Baptist's

These sinful dances caused many fights and now and then even a human life, so that it would be right for the authorities to do away with them. But just try to do away with them! Our spiritual shepherds speak against them, but the lords of the castle are more interested in ducats than the divine word!

Jurij convinced me to go, and in the afternoon we set out for Sestranska Village. We rode. Agata also mounted with me, for the valley had by now become used to it and was no longer scandalized if a woman sat next to a man on a horse. Such saddles were common in the English lands, as I later found out; but mine was made by the saddler in Škofja Loka, and he charged me a good deal for it.

As we arrived in Sestranska Village, the public was already swarming about the Čadež beer hall. There was steady dancing on all three floors, so that Janez Tičnik had a great deal to do in order not to overlook a dancer, each of whom had to pay his soldo for a turn. Whoever wanted to pay more could do so, and this was considered an honor for the girl he brought to the dance floor.

Tables and benches were set up around the floors. I chose a table for us at which several lords and their ladies were sitting. They received me gladly, particularly those who had daughters to marry off.

And Sestranska mission considered it something of an honor to allow us to dance on their floor.

Agata sat down beside me, and Jurij went to see the dancers and his friends. There was much hollering and hooting, as there always is on such sinful occasions.

I myself did not even know how to dance. But Jurij asked Agata a few times, and she danced so much that her cheeks were burning.

The lords and I spoke about various things, mostly the high taxes and other obligations that the authorities were yoking us with. We did not pay any attention to the dance or to the young people raging around the floors.

Then a voice was heard: "The rejnata is coming!" There was a ford in the Sora just below the Čadež pasture, where the dancing was going on. Passing through the water at the ford on a beautiful and lively little horse was an elegant lady, and trailing her was a giant servant with two pistols in his belt. He too was seated on a beautiful, well-fed horse. A wondrous sight for this country and for the lowly commoners who had gathered there!

However, no one was surprised, because it so happened at almost every dance that Ana Renata, of whom I have already made some mention in another place, would ride in from "Schefferten" for. She was an attractive woman, strong and also not too haughty! It was said that she had inherited a great deal from her uncle, who was bishop of Ljubljana and lame in both legs, so that he had to be carried to St. Nicholas Church if he were to take part in holy Mass. In spite of this she spoke pleasantly to everyone, even the lowliest person, and the entire valley as far as Žiri knew and loved her. But she was only pleasant as long as she was treated decently. If at a dance or after a dance some young stripling wanted her to grant him some special rights, she immediately responded with her whip, which she did not put aside even in a dance. The bold fellow could feel lucky if she did not draw him a few thick klobasas across his face.

People told how Ana Renata was stronger than her servant and how, if he would lag behind her, she would smack the hired man so hard that he saw stars. Even

Ana Renata dances

146

during the week, though she was a bishop's relative, you could see her at various types of labors. You could catch sight of her with oxen carting a basket of manure and dumping it onto the grainfield with her own hands.

I do not know the reason why the rich clan compelled her to live alone in the lonely Schefferten manor like that; nor did I ever ask about it. She was at once lord and lady, and good as both. During the week she worked but on Sundays and holidays she wanted to dance. What a woman!

She got down from her horse like the most adroit rider, causing the mountaineers simply to gape. She approached, whip in hand, having left her horse to the servant, and stopped before our table. She measured those gathered with her eyes, not haughtily, yet so as to show that she sensed her noble rank. She recognized me, stepped closer, and asked: "Will you dance, Izidor Khallan?"

Then Stefan Ramovš, a still completely immature boy from the Lučen company of young men, came up to her. Since he was the son of a rich peasant not subject to the tithe and villeinage, he was allowed to dance on the Holy Cross floor. And that animal dared to force himself on an elegant girl, saying: "Go on, have a drink, the 'rejnata,' then we'll take a turn or two!" He hooted a bit, like a young rooster that crows on the midden in the middle of the yard.

But he suddenly lost his breath, because Ana Renata looked at him contemptuously. Then she said, even more contemptuously: "At our place ones like that are still tending goats!" She cracked her whip in the air, and

147

Stefan had to jump away quick so as not to be hit. "Here are two libre, buy yourself something at the church!" She searched her clothing for the money, but Stefan, ashamed, disappeared amidst the loud laughing of the whole company.

Once more she asked: "Will you dance a little, Izidor?" I told her that I did not know how to dance, which did not suit her in the least. Then she cornered my brother: "And will you, Jurij?"

He, on the other hand, was quite forward in such matters. His eyes sparkled and he answered with satisfaction: "I do like to dance!"

She added: "I will pay the fiddlers, you understand!"

That was not in fact the custom with us, because it was the male partner had to pay "the fiddlers," but Ana Renata had her own customs. She looked for a silver Venetian crown and threw it to the fiddlers, so that Janez Tičnik was extremely pleased. He immediately cleared the Holy Cross floor, because Ana Renata's silver crown had bought her the right to one dance on the floor by herself.

The two of them danced as if they had been made for one another, and at our table the ladies of the valley whispered that never had such a pair danced at the wine festival at St. John the Baptist's. She danced with him almost the whole afternoon and would not even let him out of her arms; you could read on the conceited whelp's face how proud he was of his elegant partner!

They picked their own special table at which she paid for the drinks, so that anyone who wanted to could drink. It was near our table, and every word could be heard by us. We heard how Ana Renata praised my brother's dancing, and he loudly said again and again that his partner was the comeliest girl in the world. She did not strike him with her whip but answered nicely: "And you are the most handsome fellow in all in the valley!" It would have been no wonder if my poor brother got quite drunk simply from acting like a puffed-up bumpkin!

In the meantime, I forgot about Agata. She was sitting next to me like a chick who had been separated from her hen. All of a sudden she took me by the hand and said, "We're going home, Izidor!"

I noticed that she was pale, and, since she was frail of body, I thought that she was sick. I immediately saddled the horse and while doing so I reminded Jurij that it was time to saddle up and head off for home.

Jurij and Ana Renata answered in one voice: "Who's going to go home so soon!"

And Jurij added somewhat carpingly: "I'm going to dance as long as I want! And I'm not so young anymore that I wouldn't know the way to Visoko myself, even at night!"

Ana Renata affirmed: "And it will be night when we come by!"

And they danced again...

As Agata and I rode from Gorenja Village to Poljane she did not utter so much as a word. Now and then she sighed lightly, which I did not like. Sometimes the horse went faster, and the girl involuntarily pressed against me, and I felt this. I was overwhelmed by temptation. I too had drunk a little too much wine, which warms a man's blood, and so, forgetting that I was the master, I uttered the question: "Why do you sigh, Agata? If you aren't well, perhaps we should stay in Poljane?"

"Why wouldn't I be well?" she answered. "...you don't really think that I'd be unwell because Jurij was dancing with that elegant whore?"

These sharp words astonished me. "You may not call her a whore! She's from a good house; her uncle was a bishop, which is no trifle. In Loka I heard that the Skarlikijevs are a quite respected and rich family that has another estate besides Schefferten."

She answered coldly: "As far as I'm concerned she can carry on with all the men in the Poljane Valley— what do I care?"

From Poljane we turned up the trade road towards Visoko.

Then I began: "Jurij is frivolous and would hardly be fit to become master of an estate like mine."

She offered bitingly: "Then let him marry into Schefferten—what do I care!"

To which I replied: "And I won't have any choice but to bring a wife to Visoko. I won't be able to remain without a lady."

She began crying: "Don't I manage well for you?"

"Just because of that I would like you to become my true lady— my bride and my wife, Agata!"

My failed courtship of Agata She moaned something, so that I turned to look at her. She put an arm around my shoulders, or else she would have tumbled from the saddle. She opened her mouth a little and timidly raised her eyes, and I could see what a great quandary my words had put her in.

"In the name of the loving Lord Jesus," she sighed, "I beg you, Izidor, never to say something like that to me again! I have nothing. You cannot bring a beggar girl to Visoko!"

The words were already on my tongue to explain to her in a sensible way that her grandfather had loaned my father a great deal of money and had not returned that money, and that now at least half of both Visoko holdings were hers. I thought to myself in time that such things are not spoken and that an opportunity would come for Agata and I to talk. If she did pleaded nothing but poverty, it all could be worked out. I could certainly wait a few more years for Agata to grow older and stronger.

After this we rode home in silence. Jurij returned late at night.

The next morning I lay in bed a bit longer because I was tired from the wine. When I got up, Agata was greasing the oven for bread. It seemed to me that she was talking to someone in front of the oven.

I approached along the wall. At that moment I made out that it was Jurij speaking: "Don't be mad, Agata!"

She answered him haughtily: "I don't know why I should be mad!"

Jurij also said: "I won't dance with the one from Schefferten anymore!"

She laughed: "As far as I'm concerned you can dance with the executioner from Ljubljana! Leave me in peace, and that's that!"

I stepped from behind the wall up to the oven. Agata immediately bent down, grabbed some brushwood and threw it onto the fire. Jurij left without a word. He deserved it—that the girl had driven him off so firmly!

We endured the winter. The autumn was beautiful and long, thus we stored up thatch and fuel in order and easily got by in the cold. Nothing extraordinary happened to us, only unimportant things that were soon forgotten.

The late bishop Albrecht Sigismund had his brother's daughter, Eva Magdalena, at the castle in Loka. She was a thin woman of about thirty. She liked to go to church; but we never found out whether she knew how to do anything. She was probably a bother to the high lord, and he surely wrote to the castle magistrate many times asking him to try to marry her off to some castle. The castle magistrate worked as hard as he could settle her with some wealthy family, but Eva Magdalena remained single, because none of the manor people wanted to have her. She had a large nose and a small dowry, as bishop Albrecht Sigismund did not want to agree to any more than five hundred gold pieces. Moreover, he was not at all clear on whether those were German or domestic coin, which you can tell apart right away. I did not know Eva Magdalena personally and I never saw her in my life. Therefore I am not sure whether her nose was really as long as they say.

At Christmas, the town scribe, Konrad Fuehrnpfeill, visited me. I had fostered a certain familiarity with this lord because he was useful to me in certain ways. And he was glad to visit Visoko and never left empty handed, for such lords as have little pay and many children are happy to receive something.

Thus, when lord Fuehrnpfeill came to Visoko that Christmas, he hinted to me, after long digressions, that Eva Magdalena would like to have me. That would endear me to the lord castle magistrate, he said, and the illustrious lord bishop would not raise any objections either. But I would not be talked into it because I did not want to take Eva Magdalena, even if the baron of the castle became good and angry; I was also certain that it was precisely he that had sent the scribe to me.

My brother Jurij must have also found out about all this; perhaps the scribe himself let on to him. The family found out too and over the winter often laughed about the suit. They blabbered things that were not proper, since they had no business interfering in my affairs. Furthermore, I also noticed that Agata laughed still louder from that time on and now and then she looked at me quite wonderfully, which served as comfort. I can even write that at that time my heart was still full of love for that happy and diligent girl, and that at that time I had already firmly resolved that she would become my lady or no one else's. Since the time my brother Jurij danced so often with Ana Renata, he was no longer friends with Agata, and she hardly looked at him any longer, which was fine, and a comfort to me.

153

"He's healthy alright, but he's miserable, and there's no getting on with him."

He was about to say something more, but I did not let him, because there was probably something in it that the family ought not to hear. Therefore, I invited him first to eat his fill and, later, to tell me all he wanted. He ate for three and maybe more persons.

When the family left, Marks, Jurij, and I remained at the table to drink some wine, something that could not be neglected if a relative came to the house!

Marks told us a great deal: how Jeremija Wulffing was as old as the earth, how he clung to his farm like a tick to a dog's tail, and how he wanted his children to just toil and toil for him. He, Marks Wulffing, was getting older and there was not a holding he would not dare take over and manage sensibly. He already had a bride picked out too, who would like to come to Davča, not as a servant girl, of course, but as a wife, who gives orders to the servants. Neither did he want to be an unpaid farmhand any longer, as he had already told his father. The latter would not be budged, for he was stubborn, as every German boss is stubborn, be he old or young. So he and his father had a nasty quarrel, and, to put it all plain and simple, he left his father's home. If he had to be a farmhand, he could do so for other people and not at his father's, where he barely earned enough for clothes. If I wanted to hire him, he would stay at my place. If not, we would find himself work elsewhere.

I knew that such anger soon cools and that in a fortnight Marks Wulffing would hit the road again. So I took him into my service and promised him the pay of a first hand, with a bonus, so that at any moment he could return to his father, lest the latter think I was trying to cause discord between him and his son.

That is how Marks Wulffing arrived. But he brought misfortune with him—indeed, the worst kind that can be brought into a house…

A fortnight passed, but he was making no preparations to leave. He undertook his work with great ardor and was a first hand the likes of which I had not had before that time.

When three weeks had passed, his sister Margareta came for him, but he hid from her, so she did not even see him. She was an even more beautiful girl than before, but she did not move me at all, because by then I was already intent on Agata, who was perhaps no more pretty than Wulffing's daughter, but who had, however, been my betrothed.

Margareta comes for Marks

We had a small, narrow bench in front of the house at Visoko, and, when she was leaving that day, Margareta and I sat down on it.

"At our house," she begain lamenting, "at our house there's nothing but quarrels, and it's good that Marks isn't home because he and Othinrih had bloody fights almost every day."

"One must suffer in life," I consoled her. "How much I had to suffer with my father!"

"I know, I know," she hastened, "still it's hard."After a little while she asked, "Do you still have the little handkerchief I gave you?"

When I nodded, she complained, "How could you forget me like that!"

"Margareta," I answered, "man isn't the master of his life. If you climb to the top of a tree, you are high in the sky. Should a branch break beneath you, you fall to earth and are broken, perhaps you die. A branch broke under me, and now I'm no longer the master of my life."

"What can I say," she sobbed, "but I can't forget you."

We parted calmly, but she was almost unable to speak and tears as large as hazelnuts streamed from her eyes. She told me once again that she would wait for me and that her wait would, perhaps, be rewarded.

And indeed she did! Such was God's will, which in the end makes everything right and has mercy on each beggar. And who was a greater beggar than I, who was the master of both holdings at Visoko!

Marks stayed at the house, but he was strangely changed. He was humble and obedient, thus pleasing me, the master, and the family. He was also very talkative and could tell many stories. When we were sitting at the table there was always plenty of laughter.

I cannot write that Marks had been contending in any way for Agata. When he spoke with her it was as with any other woman. In spite of this, the maiden was open to his jokes and, if he grew silent, she begged, "Marks, tell us something more!" And once again Marks joked and Agata laughed, so that the little room quite rang!

Now and then it happened that she chatted with Marks in German, as is the custom in the place of her birth. We did not understand a thing, but the one from Davča understood everything. During this foreign talk, which contained nothing at all, something darted from

Marks's eyes, and straight at the maiden. Nonetheless, even in that I noticed nothing wrongful, because happy people like to exchange glances, which is certainly not sinful. I thought it good, too, that the maiden was so content and that she forgot about the lands where she had come into the world.

My brother Jurij was not happy about this chatting. If Marks and Agata began speaking German, he always fell silent and uttered not a word. He would stay seated a while and then leave the table, even if the last dish had not yet been brought. Such behavior seemed childish to me, for my brother Jurij should, after all, have known that Agata did not care for him and that the maiden was not intended for him!

Autumn came, after it winter, and the one from 1694 to 1695 was especially hard and bad. So much snow fell that people did not even go to Mass, and in the outlying churches there was no holy liturgy at all, because neither the priest nor anyone else could get to the divine service on account of the drifts. We lived on our stores; what work there was we did quickly and easily. We sat at meals for endless hours, and it was good that we had Marks, who amused us with his chatter.

There was plenty of snow but the roads only became slick and rutted; even in the hills, snow trails formed on which it was handy to walk.

The spinning bees commenced. Most famous was the bee at the house of our neighbor Jakob Debelak. It was very well attended and maidens even came with their accompanying men from the distant settlements of Gabrška Mountain and the Mountain of St. Sobota.

They would light torches when returning late at night, so that from afar it looked like a yellow snake was winding along the trails.

The Debelaks' was close to our place, and therefore Agata and the girls never missed a bee. When the little company was leaving there were some angry looks because Marks and Jurij quarreled over who would carry the girl's spinning wheel. Agata decided that one time Jurij would carry it, the next time Marks. The latter was not content with the verdict and he pointed out that it was the servants' right to carry the spinning wheels, and that sons of the house do not have that right, for it would be wholly improper for them to do servant work. The decision was sensible, yet both of them, Jurij and Marks, made long faces until I affirmed the girl's words. Most of all I would have liked to carry the wheel myself, which, however, would have been a great wrong, since it violates all decorum for a master to visit a bee, all the more so if he were to carry wheels for the spinners. You see, evil tongues are never at peace, and ugly talk arises overnight, leaving you tangled in a web, not yourself knowing the how or when.

In truth, nothing out of the ordinary occurred during those bees at the Debelaks'. There was no talk of them in the valley, and even the pastor never said a word to me about them, for Jakob Debelak was a pious man, who would surely not allow improprieties beneath his roof.

After Candelmas, when the forty-day fast was to begin, the bee had to break up. "Today we will break up the bee," remarked Marks at supper, "and we agreed that the wine is mine."

"So, Izidor," he said, "prepare me a cask of good wine and later put it down as a charge against my pay, if it is alright with you."

It was alright with me, because it was the custom that at the time when the bee broke up, one person would see to the wine, another to other necessities. Therefore, I prepared a cask of good wine; Marks and a servant already delivered it to the Debelaks' in the afternoon.

Others brought dry meat and also white buns; the boys from Log hired two fiddlers, and Debelak himself slaughtered a ram because he did not want to be remiss.

Thus we lived, even though the God's rod constantly hung over us.

The emperor had troops at all ends of his realm and human blood flowed in rivers over lands that were foreign to us, and where we had nothing to gain. And in order to field an army, the emperor took the holy images from our churches and turned them into money. He would not stop! And precisely in those days talk spread in the valley that they would take every fifteenth man from us, for it was said that lord Eugenius needed forces.

But we slaughter rams, we bake white buns, and even players pipe for us, so we can whirl in sinful dance! Yet how many years had there been when our housewives had nothing but grass to put in the pot. The Lord God is right to keep on beating us!

Barely had it grown dark—we had just enough time left to eat supper—when already the players showed up at Debelak's. My family almost flew to the neighbor's, but each had carelessly done his chore earlier, and I had to look over everything myself, to see whether the cattle and small livestock had gotten what they should have, and whether some fire had not been left burning that would have led to a misfortune.

A little before ten I arrived at the Debelaks'. Not a soul was left at our place. I had carefully locked all of the doors, lest a thief get at my riches. However, one still could have gotten in because a building cannot be bolted well enough to prevent an evildoer from crawling in if he really wants to steal others' belongings.

Thus in those days my heart was set on worldly belongings, and the most important thing, which had the most worth for me, was the title of master of Visoko. I surrounded that title with the frame of my conceit, as a beautiful picture is set in a gold frame and hung in the most prominent place in the house. Like Moses's golden calf, that title preceded me every moment and I brought it offerings until the Lord Jesus came and broke both the calf and me into little pieces! I was so punished, first of all because I did not know that man is only dirt in God's hand and that it is ludicrous if he is not humility itself in life; secondly, because I did not know that our most holy faith is pure love through and through: therefore, if you have any doubts, always choose the side of love, naked and pure love! Because I did not know all of that, the master of the world trampled me and like tiny grains, casting me into the dust on the road, so that the heavy wagons of life rolled over me.

When I entered at the Debelaks', the bee had almost ended. The splinters still burned brightly in their iron hoops, but only a few spinners were yet driving their wheels, the few who were not among the most comely and for whom the unwise male sex cared too little.

They were dancing. The table was set as for a wedding banquet. The wine was flowing and had already gone to certain empty heads. You could already hear the drunk mountain boys' insipid talk, from which brawls so readily arise.

Marks was his old self today, just as he was that day when he wanted to go at it with Lukež and me. During the dancing he reached for the most comely girls and, if he knew that one of them had a boy, he danced particularly long with her, which incited anger and ill will. He talked overly much. He wanted to tell everyone what to do, and if they would not listen to him, he nevertheless did what seemed fitting to him. He exposed the Tajčar, who is crude and haughty when he thinks that everyone is afraid of him.

After ten o'clock, Marks demanded his own dance. Since it was his wine that was being poured, this dance had to be granted to him, as that was the old custom.

He chose Agata, who looked particularly wonderful that day with her golden braids and her red cheeks, as his partner. I liked her so much that I simply could not take my eyes off of her. So Marks took her and stood beside her. "Now, little calves, watch how we dance, we Tajčars!" he yelled brashly. The local youths stood to the side and watched with furious eyes, but did not dare say anything in reply because they were drinking his wine.

He offered the girl his arm and the two of them danced, the likes of which we had never seen in that valley. I for one was not pleased with that leaping, but the girls' faces lit up when Marks Wulffing leapt especially high during the dance. Indeed, he jumped as if someone were stabbing him in the thigh with a knife. At times his body even flipped over, so that his legs strove towards the ceiling and his head towards the floor. When we thought that he was just about to strike it on the floor, he turned in a flash and stood on his feet once again.

Our girls liked that whirling. In the clutch that had gathered about me were daughters of wealthy peasants from the highlands, and they remarked meaningfully among themselves that Marks was not a farmhand, but the son of a wealthy farmer from Davča. Everything pointed to Marks having a clear path to the farmers' daughters, who in our times could not marry servants.

But Marks did not give those women a thought; he even forgot about the one he had already picked for himself at home in Davča. Instead, he forced himself upon Agata all the more. He talked to her a great deal, but she would not answer him, nor was she smiling any longer, as dancers are wont to do at every silly word from their partner. They were dancing more calmly. They clapped their hands a while and walked around one another as if they could not wait to come together again. At last Marks could not restrain himself any longer. He seized her around the waist, lifted her high above his head and turned with her, so that Agata's white skirts rustled. In an instant he brought her down, embraced her, and rubbed his bearded face against hers, so that I was filled with great anger.

"You're mine," he shouted like one possessed, "mine and no one else's!" He looked around like a bull in the pasture. "Let someone take her from me if you dare!" he added and sized up Jurij and his comrades. He also measured me with that look, causing—be I ten times master—the blood to boil in my body.

But Agata was not pleased with such a suit. She resisted and, because he simply would not stop pressing her to himself, we saw her raise her hand and begin to flick it across his hairy face, making a cracking sound.

"Let me go!" she said sharply, "let me go. Who can stand you, you ugly monster!"

That small blow took all of Marks's strength, for a young man loses all his repute when a woman has beaten him. He released Agata and stood in the middle of the room like a lost sheep. Laughter and guffawing surrounded him and drove him to do something most unwise at such a moment: he hissed an ugly word that was meant for everyone, and so enraged everyone.

Jurij was at him first, then the whole mob swarmed over him, which had stoked its anger that evening on account of his haughtiness. He defended himself as best he could, but they had him on the floor in an instant. They beat him and kicked him with their heavy soled shoes. They would have killed him had Debelak and I not rushed in and thrown off all who were hanging on him like bees when they attack a sweaty horse.

He moaned and groaned as he rose with difficulty. Marks Wulffing was a horror to look at: clumps of hair had been pulled from his head, his clothes were ripped; as he slowly crawled to his feet, it turned out that he was limping on one leg, and big drops of blood spurted from his face and arms. In spite of this, so much anger and so much wild hate was revealed on that face that afterwards I saw something similar only among the Turks when we put the prisoners in rows and cut off their heads!

"You got me," he complained, "because there were too many of you! Like ants you all turned on one! But what burns me worst of all is that a woman beat me—a woman who is of our people! May the devil take you all!"

With that wish, which certainly came from his heart, he hobbled off.

Thus the bee at the Debelaks' was broken up sometime after Candlemas in the year 1695.

The next morning Marks Wulffing had disappeared. The night took him; he did not even demand his pay.

Spring came and we quickly forgot about Jeremija's son. There was work in the fields, we were very diligent and did not have time to think about anything else. Agata, too, was at every chore, merry and in good humor, and we, the master and his family, liked her more each day. I did not notice anything between her and Jurij, since I knew earlier that the boy would cast these and similar whims from his head.

It was around Whitsuntide and the sun shone very beautifully. I was standing in front of the house and, when I looked towards the Debelaks' footbridge, two Loka beadles were crossing it, each with a long lance on his shoulder. In front of them strode the castle jailer, Mihol Schwaiffstrigkh. I was sure I was not mistaken: it could be none other than Schwaiffstrigkh, because he carried a large bag on his back that he never left at home when carrying sealed papers about the valley. An uneasy presentiment assailed me that these three were coming to our place and bringing nothing good with them.

In the front hall the two servants put aside their lances and leaned them against the wall. Schwaiffstrigkh began merrily: "You'll give us something to eat, Izidor, we're really hungry! That 'Flekte' roused us from our beds at break of day, and so we had to set out without having fortified ourselves."

The two servants were silent. But it seemed strange to me, the way these two men stared at our Agata, just as if they were afraid she would flutter off on them.

If the beadle is present, then there is no happiness among country folk. Therefore, there was little talk while we ate. I did ask Mihol about the Loka news. He thought a bit and then answered slowly:

"The best news is that in a week our new lord bishop, Joannes Franciscus, who just took power, is coming. He wants to look over his Loka holdings, and I surely wouldn't envy the magistrate if everything is not in order. But how can everything be in order when I know that that devil stuffs everything he can into his beggar's sack!"

When we had eaten the family went about its chores and with them the two castle servants. It seemed to me that Schwaiffstrigkh nodded something to them, at which they both quickly rose. At the window I saw that the two beadles were walking with the family and Agata to the fields. They had with them their long lances.

Mihol wanted to talk with me a bit. "How's it going?" he began. "Did you make any profit last year?"

I answered that it was not much, that the harvest was not unusual. "But there was still something left over," he responded curtly, reaching for his bag and putting it on the table in front of me. "We're paupers in town: we don't plow, and we don't sow, and neither do we reap."

Then I already knew that he had something special to tell me, and that what he was saying was not that which he wanted to say. I was afraid that it would be something bad.

He began again: "These are strange times. Sins are committed, and woe to us were there no justice at the castle!"

He looked serious and, as if by chance, he also mentioned, "I would buy a ham if it were to be had around here, and some flour. God knows I'm in need of it!"

Always giving and more giving—even the wealthiest of masters gets sick of it! Schwaiffstrigkh noticed that I did not like his words and he did not touch on the former demand. He looked out the window and began to speak:

"It will be time for us to leave if we want to get to Loka while it's day. Call Agata!"

"For what?!" I asked, and my knees were already shaking.

"She'll have to go with us," answered Mihol dryly. "They want to have her in the castle, but I don't think it's anything bad."

I grabbed Schwaiffstrigkh's bag in fear, ran off with it to the storehouse, and filled it with everything he had wanted to have before.

I begged and the man also promised me that he would deal with the girl humanely in jail.

I sent Jurij for Agata. The whole family ran up to the house with her and, when it was learned that they were

168

going to take Agata away, everyone cried. Only the maiden was calm; not even when the servants tied her hands did she lose courage. She gave the maids orders that they not forget about this and that, that they not use too much butter, that they take care that Jurij's and my things were washed and ready in good time.

She worried but little about herself. She had gathered a few rags into a bundle, which Jurij carried while I carried Schwaiffstrigkh's bulging bag. We accompanied her to Loka, for a young girl cannot be left in the hands of crude servants, who are not hesitant in lonely places and in the dark.

As we were walking, people came out of their huts and asked: "Jesus, what did she do?" Shame went with us and we talked but little on that sad walk.

I beseeched Schwaiffstrigkh to treat Agata well and not to cause her extra difficulties in the jail. He promised me and repeated: "Izidor, don't worry yourself! What can it be? Some small thing, some lying gossip of the Poljane hags. If it were worse, believe me, it would not be kept secret from me, because the lord magistrate tells me all that is most important."

After a short silence he added: "But since you're in Loka anyway, it wouldn't hurt for you to go to the lord baron, so that he will treat Agata gently!"

But I could not get it into my head to grovel before "Flekte," who had thrown me into the stocks. So strong was worldly pride in me at that time!

I should also write this: When we came to the first houses in Zminec, the sky grew dark and of a sudden it rained hail as thick as chicken eggs. We were just able to take cover. The hail flattened the fields and the green-wood from Brodi to Loka town. It pounded the crops, which were growing nicely, into the earth, and from some it took their bread, so that they suffered later that winter.

We turned Agata over to the castle in the dark of night. I immediately set off for home, but Jurij stayed in the town. Later Schwaiffstrigkh told me that the next day my brother went to the castle magistrate's wife and begged her on his knees to take up the poor girl's cause and defend her from the crude servants. Jurij told me nothing of that, but the lady did indeed care for the girl.

We lived in terrible times! But Jesus Christ was my first and last consolation!

XI.

The Lord's hand was upon my house! Heavy as iron and as hard as rock, set in the bowels of a mountain from the time it was created! We prayed, we assisted at divine service—but the Lord did not relent because He could not forget Jošt Schwarzkobler's bloody death! And he was so angered that He crushed the children of both men and their childrens' children, for both were great sinners, Polikarp Khallan as well as Jošt Schwarzkobler!

I do not know how many weeks later it was that my neighbor Debelak stopped before my entrance on his way from Loka. I saw that he would like to speak with me. At that time we neighbors lived together in mutual love: what hurt one, the other felt as well, and if one cried, the other did not laugh, as is likely to be the habit among the Germans. Since the time they had taken Agata away from us not much work was done at my place. We only saw to it that the livestock did not suffer and were not thirsty; in other matters, we folded our arms and secretly wiped our eyes. Neither was the master an example to others; he behaved as the family behaved.

That afternoon, when my neighbor was returning from town, I was sitting idly on the bench in front of the house. My brain was consumed with thoughts: How in the name of beloved Jesus the Christ, could she have sinned? What did Agata actually do that the law could arrest her? In church and everywhere we were taught that the law does injustice to no one! Everything was spinning in my head, everything was awhirl, so that I would have lost even the little bit of sense that the Lord God gave Visoko's sons had not my patron St. Izidor taken up my defense!

Thus Jakob Debelak stopped in front of me. I noticed that he was searching for the words that he wanted to speak. The blood had gone from his face and his lips were trembling as he tried to open his mouth. We looked at each other for a few moments and I immediately noticed that my neighbor's eyes were all watery. "The rock will break loose," I said to myself, "and as it crashed down on my father's grave, so now it will crash on me!" My neighbor composed himself and began with a forced ease:

"The new bishop arrived yesterday. Loka was in a dither. He has two names. They call him Janez Frančišek."

I knew that that was not what he wanted to tell me. I fixed my gaze on his troubled face and did not answer.

"He was coming in the Water Gate," said Debelak, "and the elders greeted him. He's called Janez Frančišek, I'm telling you."

"Did you hear anything about our girl?" I stammered fearfully.

I was not blind and saw that it was just on account of the girl he had come to see me. He looked skyward and the words came to him with difficulty.

"Just wait and I'll tell you! I met the town scribe on the square, you know him after all, Lord Boltežar. And he ordered me to tell you… Just wait and I'll tell you…" Beads were gathering on his forehead. "What was it he ordered me to do? Just wait and I'll tell you… The new bishop arrived, and Lord Boltežar, who is your friend, advised that you go before the bishop. It would go well and it won't do any harm…"

"On account of… the girl?" I stammered.

"Fuehrnpfeill says that it's on account of the girl! Wait, exactly on account of the girl, and that it won't hurt…"

"Does the bishop bother himself with such trifles?" I asked uncertainly.

"Fuehrnpfeill says that he does!"

I sobbed, "For God's sake, just what do they have against the girl?" The answer was slow in coming. Debelak turned to look in all directions and he ran his fingers through his gray hair. He finally replied glumly: "They accuse her of having caused the hail, of riding your pigs above your house, and of making love to the devil."

Neighbor Debelak relates terrible things, and that a pyre is being put up on Gavžnik

I shot up. The blood started to boil in me and the world fell to pieces around me!

"Jesus Christ!—Are they idiots!—Our Agata, my Agata…"

Jakob calmed me: "Just wait and I'll tell you—I don't know a thing. Fuehrnpfeill says that Marks is giving some sort of evidence and that he wants to testify…"

"Marks Wulffing?!" I shouted. Something burst inside of me and as if from afar I heard my neighbor's voice: "Fuehrnpfeill says to hurry, he says that the executioner has already come from Ljubljana, that they are already putting up a pyre on Gavžnik…"

A dark cloud covered me. I fell to the ground and had a sense of flying into a deep abyss.

When I awoke I was lying in the upper house and they were daubing my head with water. I had been lying in my bed for two days or more and did not recognize the world around me. I was turned toward the ceiling and before my poor soul stood… Agata, with her sweet face beneath a golden crown of golden braids, and she had two eyes that shone with virgin innocence. For that woman the heart of Visoko's master yearned! Since she had been gone I missed her every day; and at every step I took, something within sighed for her to whom I was inseparably bound by the spilt blood of Jošt Schwarzkobler! Each moment I thought of her, who was destined for me. And now? What had Fuehrnpfeill said? They locked her up because she made love to the devil and she committed sins such as wicked witches commit??? I would toss about on my bed the whole night long and the whole night I would pray to Our Lady of Gora to grant me the favor of finding out whether there are witches in the world or not. My dear Savior, Jesus, help me! But everything screamed to me that there were witches, for otherwise they would not have been burning them on pyres for centuries and up to the present day! And yet I also knew that they burned them only after they themselves would remorsefully admit everything. There are witches—that I can say; but that Agata was not a witch—that, too, I write, for Jesus in His glory would surely not have destined Polikarp's son to make recompense for the blood of a murdered man in that way! Holy Godhead—and if, after all, she was! So many sins are committed throughout our land that only the Creator knows all of them. And should the Visoko master enter into marriage with one who, perhaps, flew to Slivnica near Cerkno or even to Klek in Croatia! Saint Izidor, come to my aid lest I lose my mind, lest my reason dry up and all understanding abandon me!

I was like a broken branch washed into the Sora in a flood: The water bears it along and it cannot stop. Such a branch was my soul. God's wrath hurried it along and nowhere could it stop!

On the fourth of August, on the feast of St. Dominic Guzmán, I had recovered enough to set out for Loka at the break of day when there was as yet neither horse nor man on the road. No one was showing his face then, even in the huts, and thus I could hide from all living things, for shame had come upon the house and I had to look at the ground and nowhere else. I followed the words: "If a man would come after me, let him deny himself and take up his cross and follow me!" (Matthew 16:24). And it was a heavy cross I bore on my shoulders on my way to town!

Loka was still celebrating because the Škofja Lokans had the great good fortune of having in their midst the person of their wise and most kind new master. As for myself, I did not partake of that happiness and truly took fright at, the great flag that waved from the castle tower. The thought oppressed me that soon I would travel a most bitter path to that castle, to him who was a mighty and also, certainly, a hardhearted lord. As I have already said, the burghers were festively dressed and so were the menials. Yet not many of them were coming to the square, for our nature is such that we avoid high lords, even if we love them.

Mihol Schwaiffstrigkh stood in front of Wohlgemuet's tavern looking morose.

"You come to see the new bishop, too?" he asked me sullenly. He did not mention Agata at all, for which I was thankful to him, for a man does not like to talk about his misfortune with a beadle.

He added, "If he'd just soon off to where he came from!"

"Are you being wronged?" I asked.

"What can I tell you!" Schwaiffstrigkh raged. "Everything has been turned upside down at the castle, everything is a mess, and Lord Joannes Franciscus is giving commands like some Swedish general. The words he uses—you're already shaking before he says them! They say he used to be an officer before he entered the Church. Maybe he was, maybe he wasn't, but he acts like it! If you could see our 'Flekte' today! He'd shrivel up to nothing right in front of you before you could pick him out in the sand underfoot! You think I have anything to say! Even less than a rat in the cells! He brought some violet with him. 'Violet, do this' and 'violet, do that,' and we who are carrying out our honorable duty have to hold our tongues!"

He grumbled on and then he said, "I already know you won't give me anything for drink!"

He set off and one could see that he was glad to leave my company, because he probably decided that I would start asking about Agata, whose jailer he was. But I gathered from his words that my path to the castle would be even thornier than I thought. What can I say? God have mercy on me!

I waited in front of the town hall for the town scribe, Boltežar Fuehrnpfeill, to come. When he arrived, he headed for the castle and later notified me at Wohlgemuet's that with the help of the young provost he had persuaded the most merciful lord bishop to allow me to see him in his room at two, and that I could perhaps convince him not to burn Agata, who was accused of such terrible evil. This frightening message could beat me down no more, since I was already beaten into the ground!

He took his leave, saying, "Just be sure you keep your head on your shoulders, else you'll accomplish nothing! And don't be too afraid; the high lord has a sharp tongue but he doesn't think so badly! At least that's what the provost told me. So keep your courage up no matter how much Lord Joannes Franciscus screams in French!"

When he was walking away he added, "Come on time or else you're on the outs right off! After come and tell me what you accomplished."

He said that with a purpose that was not lost on me: for his services he demanded pay, which he was due and for which I already had a couple of gold coins in my pocket, but I couldn't hand them to him on the square.

At exactly two o'clock I stepped into the castle yard. There was no life to be sensed in the large edifice. Only the lord provost from St. Jakob's was marching to and

My thorny path to the Loka castle and about all I underwent with Bishop Janez Frančišek fro along the passage in front of the bishop's quarters, reading a book. It was the young lord Urh Falenič, nephew of the one-time Poljane pastor. Besides his large parish he was performing the service of castle chaplain, since his mercy had come to his castle. He noticed me and right away hurried up.

"It's good that you're on time!" he praised me, "because our lord doesn't like to wait! —Wait here a moment!"

He left me in the passageway. My heart was beating like never before in my life, because I had never spoken with a real bishop, as was the merciful lord Joannes Franciscus, who was probably not much less than the German emperor. And it was as if a sharp knife pierced my heart when I looked at the wide, black castle tower that rose just before me against the sky. The deep, dark cells in which the prisoners could not stand or lie down, opened before my eyes, and it actually seemed to me that I could hear the clanging of heavy chains. Once again I write, Jesus, have mercy on me!

Lord Urh soon returned and took me into some sort of anteroom.

He was saying: "Our lord is wondrous! In spite of all the danger, he took up residence in the room where the two servants murdered their bishop Konrad. He wants to battle people's fears and every night he sleeps on the martyr's bed. But don't worry too much, Izidor, all the same he's a good lord!"

Here he turned to some man with a heap of flax on his head and ordered him: "Valet de chambre, announce us to his illustrious mercy!"

This man was probably the "violet" Schwaiffstrigkh told me about. He approached the door with quiet steps, opened it and said something, after which he gestured to me to enter.

Lord Urh remained in the anteroom, and I went into the bishop's room, which had not changed since the time I had seen it. The cross on the wall was still there and so was the modest bed. There was a table by the window and several chairs around it. On one sat our new lord bishop.

Joannes Franciscus, how wrongly a man would judge you if he judged you by your harsh words!

I must write that I imagined the powerful master of a large bishopric differently than my eyes beheld him that afternoon. On the wide chair sat an insignificant person, as thin as a stalk in the middle of a hay field, in worn clothing that showed a great many stains, and I could have sworn that the Poljane pastors went about in better robes than the one Joannes Franciscus wore that day. What indicated an heir of the apostles was the red embroidery on the robe and the buttons, which were also red. He was not wearing a gold chain about his neck as the lord bishops usually do. However, a large gold cross could be seen between the buttons on his chest, but it was not especially adorned with precious stones. There were two small white patches around his neck that testified to his clerical station.

Such was the small likeness of our new bishop! But his tiny face, which I could have covered with my palm, nevertheless spoke for all of the bishopric. Every little feature on that face said that Joannes Franciscus was not a man to joke with. That small face, surrounded by a small gray wig, had iron features, and although his eyes looked kindly on the world, I was soon convinced that the thin mouth below his somewhat coppery nose could command just as the highest church shepherd commands his subjects. The high lord did not hide the fact that he liked the drink that is born of the green vine— that is, in moderation, and with the fondness that older, wise lords have for that fruit of the blessed land, be they of clerical or lay estate. That is to say, at that moment Lord Joannes Franciscus raised his silver goblet and slowly drank from it, savoring the worth of each drop he quaffed.

It was most probably the best Črni Kal, which was always in supply in the castle cellars for any occasion. Then his hand reached for the gilded dish that was piled with tiny whitish figs.

The merciful Joannes Franciscus was quite assiduously bearing those figs to his mouth, despite my presence. He only glanced sideways in my direction, and then he immediately reached for the dish again. Therefore, I was led to think he was not pleased that I was not yet kneeling, as is obligatory when you come before a bishop. I immediately knelt and humbly beat my breast.

At that moment the bishop turned to me and gave a shout:

"Pierre, valet de chambre!" The old man with the light step and heap of flax on his head appeared at the door and bowed deeply before his lord.

"Pierre," he said firmly, "tell this man that one does not kneel before a person! Do you think that I am

'Flekte,' for whom God made a head but forgot to make brains?" He began laughing in such a way that every feature on his little face laughed and his little eyes shone like sparks. And he repeated, "Who do you think I am, Flekte?"

When the servant disappeared, Joannes Franciscus pointed to a chair by the table: "Sit down!" This honor affected me so keenly that I did not know when and how I got to the chair.

Then he grabbed a whole fistful of figs and scattered them on the table in front of me: "Eat!" And once more the room was filled with his loud and healthy laughter.

I did not like eating before such a lord but I had to, and I could not swallow the entire mouthful. In the meantime, Joannes Franciscus shuffled some papers, then he asked: "Izidor Schwarzkobler?" *I had to eat figs, but it's not good to eat them with a high lord*

I replied, "Khallan… If you please, you may also write Khallain, your grace!"

"So, it's not your sister? Perhaps your plighted?" I could not say that, for the master of two holdings at Visoko could not admit that a woman who was in jail for witchcraft was his plighted! But I explained to the gracious lord how Jošt Schwarzkobler's granddaughter had come to my house, though I did not mention the murder that my father already had answered for at his heavenly judgment.

Lord Janez Frančišek's tiny face shrank somewhat and his eyebrows come right together when he asked, "So it's not love for the unfortunate woman that has brought you to me but love for your two holdings, which would come to shame if we condemn Agata Ema Schwarzkobler?"

I reluctantly groaned, "It's hard to live with such shame!"

The bishop laughed dryly: "I don't know what will happen! This sinful Agata Ema is accused of very terrible things. I read that she actually had conjugal relations with the devil, and I'm surprised that nothing was born of that infernal union, not even a few piglets, so she wouldn't have had to borrow them from you when she felt like riding in circles above your house! And she went right into that Marks Wulffing's flesh, and my sagacious Mändl included with the documents the flint that Marks removed from his wound with his own hand! By the saints in heaven, everything fits, everything is proven, and divine providence has sent me to this place just in time!"

Each crease on his very fine face took on a satanic expression. His small figure leapt from the chair and flew about the room causing the little robe to dance about it.

"Agata is lost!" I began quaking within and I started praying the Our Father to myself. I did not know French curses then, but later, in various engagements, I got used to them, too. Therefore, I can write that Joannes Franciscus was cursing as he galloped about the room. He was cursing in French because our forsaken Agata's proven sin so enraged him!

"Mon Dieu!" he shouted, "an *exemplum* must be set. I want to provide an *exemplum* in these lands so that they will no longer be battered by hail, and Lucifer and his brothers will no longer sow their illicit piglets among them! Parbleu!"

He complained about some Jesuit *pater* who was sleeping[*] and he said some other things that were beyond my peasant ken. Once again, he galloped up and down the room and I could clearly hear that he was grinding his teeth; his face began to burn, and he had crumpled each hand into a fist. Poor Agata!

When he calmed down a little he asked me sharply and caustically, just as if poking a sharp knife into my ear: "What's going to happen to your pigs now?"

The high lord even thought of that. "There are six of them," I replied, "and they are getting nice and fat."

"Why wouldn't they fatten well when after all a witch is giving them their slop?!" yelled the gracious lord bishop. He yelled! I cannot say otherwise, for even high lords are wont to yell when they are angered. Oh, Saint Izidor, bishop Joannes Franciscus was then angered to the fullest measure! He added, "Maybe she sat on one of them, maybe on all six! Diablo!"

"If you condemn Agata," I stammered, "the family will not want to eat them; I will kill them and bury them in the forest, where the foxes will dig them up; there are many of them in the Visoko woods. If you don't condemn her, then I will slaughter them.

The bishop laughed menacingly: "That's right! You're a sensible master, Izidor Schwarzkobler!"

"Izidor Khallan, your grace!" I humbly corrected him.

"Izidor Khallan then! An empty pot is empty, call it Schwarzkobler or Khallan!"

[*] The Jesuit Spee!

He sat down in his chair, drummed his fingers on the table and looked out the window at the plain, bathed in gold.

"The sun's shining and we have nice enough weather," he said calmly.

"The weather is good and the crop won't be bad," I responded bravely.

"The crop—that's what comes first for you!" He was tapping on the table so sharply that I did not dare answer.

The merciful Joannes-Francis-cus put a very hard question to me Joannes Franciscus was silent for quite a while, but then he quickly turned to me with a pleasant look and a light smile on his lips and addressed me thus:

"Izidor Khallan, imagine that you are at holy confession with your spiritual pastor, and imagine that I am your spiritual shepherd! Answer me this: Do you believe there are sorceresses or enchantresses or witches in the world? Answer me just as you would your God if He were to call you before Him!"

Holy Trinity, help me! That was the question I was shuddering at all the days since they had taken Agata from me! I was afraid of that question and I hoped that it would not come up. But it did, and I had to answer as I would answer the Lord, who dwells in the holy tabernacle. If Agata was damned, I did not have the right to mortgage my share in the heavenly kingdom!

The most gracious bishop watched me brightly, and I was beginning to think that his burning gaze would bore through me.

I answered: "Christ is my witness that I believe!"

"That there are witches, that there are sorceresses? Would that the Lord Jesus give me plenty of such subjects!" the high lord exclaimed. Then he asked in a hushed voice: "How do you support this belief of yours?" Again he reached for the figs in the gold dish.

But in no way did I want to become deserving of eternal damnation! "As far as I recollect," I answered, "the world has persecuted them, and the authorities have always condemned them and brought them to the pyre. But no one was burned who himself didn't first and sincerely admit infernal evildoing."

The merciful lord brought his goblet to his lips and fortified himself with a sip of sweet Črni Kal wine. When he had done so, he fixed his eyes on me so that I felt as if two pointy arrows were piercing me.

He laughed bitterly: "You're well-schooled. Perhaps you've already been in my Loka tower, where even today we have wonderful stores for getting the admissions you're referring to!"

"The authorities are mistaken here and there," I answered, "but for them to be mistaken in every case, why, it would be a sin to claim such a thing."

It now happened that one of the highest nobles of the holy Church began laughing so hard that there was reason to fear he would suffer an overwhelming seizure.

"You're right, my son, the authorities are rarely mistaken! Only it's odd that it was you who litigated again and again against Albreht Sigismund when you had been denied the right to litigate at the time of Vid Adam!"

It is easy to confuse an awkward farmer, so I was silent.

He also asked: "Isn't it odd, dear young man, if Agata is so powerful, if she consorts with the devil, who is, you can believe me, a great lord, that she doesn't help herself, flutter out the window and thus shake herself free from Loka's onerous justice?"

Here again I did not know how to answer.

He put the question once again: "What then? Do you still believe that there are witches in the world?"

Now I could but stammer, "I don't know."

Bishop Janez Frančišek does not believe in witches, which I can't believe!

"You're surely kin to Saint Thomas! Now listen to your bishop, listen to your ruler! He answers you, 'I don't believe.'" And Lord Joannnes Francsiscus got up and flew about the little room once more.

Everything was atumble in my head and I perceived nothing but the crucifix that signified the bitter death of blessed bishop Konrad. Despite this my conceit was not yet erased and my heart still cried out that the master of Visoko could not take a woman that had been dragged through the Loka cells because of witchcraft.

"If you're able," screamed the bishop, "open your ears and listen! We're going to test her by water. If by any means—by any means—Agata comes out of the water alive, her innocence is proven."

He pronounced the words "by any means" twice and put special stress on them. But in vain, for my head would not clear, and so I did not know whether those words were meant to convey anything special.

My feebleness did not go unnoticed by the bishop. He stopped by me and disgustedly pronounced these words: "You want to rescue the sinner? You want to rescue her from the pyre? You won't rescue her! You're a…" He thought it over for a while and then he added very frankly, "You're a dunce!"

186

At that bitter word I crumpled and broke into such a sweat that the clothes I was wearing became wet. Since I had been the master of both Visoko holdings I had not been stung by a word like the one that the magnificent lord bishop Janez Frančišek hurled at me that moment! Such words are appropriately directed at a servant, but never at a master, even if he does not have as many fields or as many pack horses as I have altogether at Visoko!

"Valet de chambre!" he called out. The old man with the huge wig entered. "Pierre, take this man out!"

I left as if drunk and so forgot to pay the homage that the whole world pays to the heirs of the apostles!

Perhaps I was mistaken, perhaps I heard correctly—at the door it seemed to me that I heard laughter from his grace. It was poisonous laughter, but then I did not yet know Janez Frančišek's golden heart that was hidden behind that laughter and the blessed benevolence that was in every drop of blood flowing through his frail body!

That day I left the Loka castle with the knowledge that the Freising bishop did not want to help us.

On the way back from Loka my soul wept and I thought of her who was in chains and whom I did not have the courage to visit. I thought of her… but the rich grain fields and green Visoko meadows, all of which were my property, also lay before my eyes. Now and then something stirred in a far corner of my soul: Should I take a woman who was to be tried before the whole world? When God abandons a man he is like a flag that is forever flapping in the direction the wind blows!

My brother Jurij was waiting for me in front of our home. He had simply withered during these days, so that there was almost nothing left of him in his clothes.

"Were you with her?" he asked.

"I was with the bishop," I answered, "but I didn't dare ask him to let me see her. He was like a thorny bush that you don't put your hand into."

"Did he say anything about her?" he asked very worriedly.

"He said something about wanting to test her by water, and if she comes out of the water alive—that is, by any means—then her innocence is proven. But how can a man know what's what in the speech of high lords, who are so fond of mocking us poor peasants!"

Jurij walked away.

Afterwards we lived on. We lived like a flock on Blegoš, from which a bear has carried off the most beautiful ewe!

At the end of July Schwaiffstrigkh again came to Visoko. He came as an emissary of the court (Weisbot) and brought me and Jurij sealed papers. They were summoning us to Škofja Loka on the eleventh day of August, the day of St. Tiberius Martyr, for us to testify at the hearing, when Agata Ema Schwarzkobler would be tried for most evil witchcraft.

XII.

The inquest was to begin at ten o'clock in the morning on the feast of St. Tiberius Martyr. Jurij and I rode to town bright and early. We hoped we would be alone and not be forced to cast our eyes down, since after all the whole valley from Žiri to Loka knew and was talking about our shame. But we were sorely deceived: there was almost as large a throng on the road as goes on pilgrimages. Hill folk and valley dwellers—there were plenty of both, and some of them were so lacking in any sense that they were even dragging children along. Everyone was hurrying to town and there were almost more than the day they beheaded the fellow from Ferrari's regiment who had murdered and robbed a peasant from Zminec. They left us in peace, even the ones that were convinced that Agata was a witch because last year hail had fallen here and there in the highlands and valley.

How are Agata appeared before the blood-thirsty judges in Loka

Ana Renata of Schefferten was setting out too, since the servant was leading two saddled horses in front of the manor. We doubled back around a knoll and waited for Ana Renata to ride out with her servant. We intentionally let the people go ahead and pass us so that we were among the last when we rode into town through the Poljane Gate.

We put our horses under Wohlgemuet's roof but there was almost no one home since almost everyone was at the trial. Loka, too, was empty. Everyone was rushing to the place where Janez Frančišek had ordered a full hearing, open to all.

At the bishop's command they had fenced in the area of pasture beneath the lower wall and stretching from the Poljanska to the Selška Sora, and there they would hold the hearing before the entire public, so that afterwards no one could say there was an attempt to hide something. The only thing on the meadow was the blacksmith Langerholz's shack, there was no other building in the wide space. Somewhere in the middle a square, fenced court was readied; there was a table for the judges and an elevated stage that could be seen from all four sides. Here Agata was to sit—the bishop himself had so ordered.

At nine o'clock the throng was already milling about on the pastures surrounding the court, and it was awaiting events with great curiosity. And not only on the triangular flat between the Selščica and Poljanščica, people were also jostling on the far side of both streams; especially on the right bank of the Poljanščica, on Lord Apfaltrern's meadow, they were standing man to man. The steward from Puštal was trying to drive people away because the aftergrass had not been cut and they would ruin the rich, good feed for him. But he tried without any success because at nine o'clock they were already standing shoulder to shoulder on his aftergrass.

At half past nine Mihol Schwaiffstrigkh came and led us to the area where the witnesses were to wait. The space was behind the fence; he sat Jurij and me on a long wooden bench and then went away again. The citizenry surged before us just like a big river in too narrow a course. Some fifty Loka women, old and young but more old, had gathered hard by the enclosure. The town baker's wife, Urša Prekova, and the town butcher's wife, Maruša Stinglova, had the first word. Later I was told that Goodwife Urša could not bear Goodwife Maruša: the baker traded on one side of the street and the butcher on the other, so they had ample opportunity to have words daily, and for the smallest trifle. When these two quarreled Loka hurried to gather because they were well matched, and the listeners would always get some fun. But for today they had agreed to be great friends and they also brought a nice flock of other acquaintances so that their company occupied almost the entire fence. Ana Renata was also among them with her crop. I felt good when, sitting on the bench, I got the feeling that those women were not at all against Agata but on the contrary were quite plainly pulling for her.

"Have you ever heard," cried Urša Prekova, "of a dove ripping up a vulture?"

"Such a creature, and a witch!" shouted Maruša. "May the devil take those men that will judge her! Why don't they call us in for such judgments? Why? Why, I ask you!"

Then an old peasant from Inharji with a long shirt and wide belt about his belly was rash enough to drawl: "You talk like that 'cause you yourself are probably afraid of landing up in her place!"

I cannot describe what a tumult arose! In a moment they had knocked the Inharec's hat off his gray head and beset him with the ugliest words from their well-stocked storehouse. And Ana Renata offered her crop to Prekova and cried: "Whack him on his dundering head so that he remembers!"

The man from Inharji would probably have been beaten bloody had not a shout gone up among the throng at that moment: "They're bringing her!"

Suddenly everyone was quiet and all eyes turned to the slope below the Poljane Gate. Down the slope was moving a small wagon in which sat our Agata. Mihol Schwaiffstrigkh guided the small horse. Two castle servants walked on each side of the wagon with long lances pointing skyward, so that it was ugly to watch.

The wagon stopped in the middle of the enclosure by the stage. I did not dare look over there lest I see her poverty, nor did I dare stand up because I was ashamed were the crowd to know that I was the master of the Visoko holdings, which claimed the present accused as its own.

I will record that my brother Jurij behaved completely differently. The wagon had barely stopped when Jurij was already standing by Agata. He called out so that it could be heard all around: "Agata, don't be afraid!" He took her thin hand in both of his and pressed it to his cheek and was not at all ashamed. The blood rushed to the poor girl's face and she ran her other hand over his curly head two or three times.

She could not get down from the wagon without another's help. Jurij took her with one hand into his grasp and with the other arm held the heavy chain about her leg. Then he carried her to the stage himself and there he sat her on the bench prepared for her. The chains jangled loudly all the while, so that great pity came over the people. Instantly a great many hands were wiping eyes, and the Loka women in front of the fence burst into loud sobbing. "Trust in God, Agata!" said Jurij as he left the stage.

Agata occupied her place, on display before the gathered crowd. In her shame she did not dare look to the right or left. She sat as if there were no life in her.

Now I glanced at her for the first time. Merciful God! She looked like a hazel twig stuck in women's clothing, her face was like wax, and her cheeks were sunken like two shallow graves. If it were not for the people I would have started crying, and I did feel how drops gathered on my eyelashes. Only once did she lift her face and look at the mountains that were right in front of her and on which the snow shown white beneath the sun's rays. It would have been better for her had she been up on the snowcap, where she would have been safe from the severity of the Loka judges, who had made her new homeland bitter! Then she lowered her gaze and fixed it continually at the board in front of her, just as if she were surprised at the heavy chain that lay on the it and bound her weary leg.

Again there was something unexpected! A strange man was pushing a wooden wheel barrow down the slope from the Poljane Gate. When he passed by, the crowd stirred in terror and drew back, quickly making a space through which a pair of harnessed horses could have driven. The man, who was powerful and had uncommonly thick arms, was pushing his wheel barrow, which he had loaded with his special things. He did not say anything, only laughed and looked sideways at the people, whom he disliked, as they disliked him. They did not look upon him long but in an instant everyone knew that it was the executioner, or as he is called in our parts, the frajman from Ljubljana.

There was a special table prepared for him, it was in a distant corner behind the fence. The disreputable man hauled his load toward that place and it must have been hard, for now and then he wiped his sweaty face with a red sleeve. As soon as he stopped—and here the crowd jumped back and gave him room—he drew from his barrow a great, red as blood cloth and covered his table with it. He used nails to fasten the cover in four spots, driving them into the table with a small hammer, so that the breeze would not disturb it. Right after that he somewhat haughtily and self-consciously took a sword out of the barrow, and it was as bare as is bare the sword in St. Michael's hand, and it burned just as the sword of the archangel burns; he took it into his grasp as a mother does an infant, considered the crowd meaningfully, and said in a repulsive voice: "He has had his sup many times and always leaves an empty plate! This child of mine eats everything that is given him!" He laughed hoarsely as he put the bare sword down, and it shone in the middle of the blood red table cloth like a big icy candle.

There was noise rose from the crowd. Curses and vulgarities were heard, and the young men were already picking up stones to throw at the table.

"No stones, boys!" Schwaiffstrigkh spoke up. "Whoever I catch will lie in the stocks until he has blisters on his back and welts in his stomach!" Glancing at the frajman, he added: "He is truly a pig but he has his rights!"

The people settled down. But the executioner cared not a wit for the commotion and noise; blithely, as if the outburst had not been meant for him, one by one from his pushcart he took the tools for tormenting male and female prisoners alike and piled them on the table until it was covered with sundry pieces of iron that gleamed unpleasantly, one more than the other!

The onlookers strained, the women shook in terror—only she continued sitting on her stage without stirring in the least, just as if she was ignorant of what that disgusting man was attending to at his red table!

It struck the tenth hour at St. Jakob's. Then the lord judges stepped up to their table with the castle magistrate, Lord Mändl, at their head. He had five assessors under him, and they were: the castle scribe, the town judge, the castle garneter, Frueberger the goldsmith, and someone else whom I no longer remember. A judge had also been sent from Ljubljana; his name has also escaped me, so I can no longer write it down today. He was a man of thin profile and in black clothing. The whole time he interfered in the proceedings and was almost more annoying than old Frueberger—may God forgive him for that day's wickedness!

The castle magistrate announced right off that by the grace of the chief of all judicial trials—that is, by the grace of lord Janez Frančišek—the public trial was to be held in such a way that each would take part in the inquest and judge whether everything had been done justly and rightly. The assembled crowd was reminded to be

195

worthy of this great favor and not to disturb the open proceedings, which were the first in the town since it was built, by causing a commotion or even tumult.

Lord Mändl wore a sour face because he did not care for that public trial at all, and he was loudly telling the fellow from Ljubljana, as I well heard from my bench, that it was not wise to call ignorant country people to be present when educated and professional judges were sitting. But he had to give in because there was no helping it against the bishop and ruler.

The castle magistrate dispersed his town guard among the people to prevent them from causing disorder and commotion. But the people in our day were devoted and submissive to the authorities, as is proper and sensible. Thus also that morning there was no occasion for the town or castle guards to display their strength. Only Urša Prekova and Maruša Stinglova could not rein themselves in and even during the trial they made noise and spoke in Agata's favor. Baron "Flekte" became enraged and was ready to throw Goodwife Maruša in jail; but provost Urh convinced him not to, arguing that the lord bishop would hardly like it if on that day the respected wives of Loka burghers were locked up in his name. The lord provost, it happens, had also come to the inquest, though he was not taking part in it. Nonetheless he was sitting at the judges' table, and it was said that afterwards he told Lord Janez Frančišek everything, and explained what had taken place and what had been said.

Baron Mändl began to shuffle some notes, then he stated that the trial against the accused was commenced, and that she was born in Eyrishouen in such and such a year and that she had been baptized in the names of the saints Agata and Ema.

"Ema," growled the judge from Ljubljana, "Ema—that isn't without meaning! We switch the first two letters and we have 'mea,' which means that already at her birth the devil had her in mind and she was his even at that moment. So her marriage with the devil was arranged even then, when Agata Ema Schwarzkobler came into the world!"

And Lord Frueberger added: "Certainly, that is extremely meaningful! That 'mea' proves almost everything."

At that point Mother Maruša turned to Mother Urša and asked:

"Why is that black Ljubljana rag butting in? And our Frueberger even! Have you ever seen two such stupid people? You hear 'May I' often enough but it doesn't prove a thing!" It was then that Baron "Flekte" was about to lock up mother Maruša and when Lord Provost Urh would not allow it.

Then they questioned Agata: Where did she first see the devil? Where did she cause the first hail? When was she at Slivnica near Cerkno, and when at Klek in Croatia? Was the pig she rode taken from her master or did Satan bring it from somewhere else?

They also wanted to know whether she had any companions who worshipped the devil along with her. Likewise, whether she forced the needle, flint, and nail into Marks Wulffing's flesh, causing his leg to swell and him to wrongfully suffer pain.

And so they asked her about a great deal, one thing more wicked than the next. But Agata did not move from her seat. Her face remained calm and it was so lovable and sweet that the assembled crowd could not get enough of it. She did not lower her gaze at all, although she did not raise her face from the ground. What she repeated unceasingly was that it was not true.

"That is a stubborn sinner," fumed Frueberger. "After all, she's from Visoko, they have hard noggins there!"

"We have aids," laughed the black judge from Ljubljana, "you'll see, noble Lord Frueberger, how her tongue will be loosened and she will tell us more than we require!" That repulsive figure laughed and it sounded as if a crow were making noise in a pine top.

But Frueberger would not let it rest and he asked the accused: "Were there any off spring from when you made love to your infernal brother, huh?"

To show it was not true, she sighed and turned red, so that everyone pitied her, especially old Neža Bergant, who roared: "You swinish pig, you!"

The people burst out laughing, Baron "Flekte" and his assessors laughed too, because they did not begrudge dirty talk to an old sinner who could not hold his tongue.

Jurij and I were heard and we testified to the truth, the pure truth. They soon returned me to the wooden bench because they noticed I was confused. They held on to Jurij longer because he was shocking and did not behave as prescribed before the judges. In particular that nightbird from Ljubljana did not want to let him out of his clutches and wanted to squeeze this and that from him.

Among other things they asked him whether he believed there are witches in the world. He bravely answered that he did not believe so. When the black one asked him why not, the answer was short: "Because I've never seen one!"

They asked further whether Jurij might have seen her riding on a pig above the roof of the house. He answered: "Never once! But we can give it a try. Come to Visoko, most esteemed lord, and I'll ready our biggest pig for you, and you can sit on it and go riding through the air, like the lords on the Ljubljana riding grounds in front of the Viceroy Gate! Then I'll tell you for certain whether I noticed anything in the air above the house or not!"

The listeners were quite pleased with that answer. Laughter resounded in the women's ranks, and, most of all, Ana Renata did not hide her glee at the answer. To me it did not seem proper or needed by any means.

The withered Ljubljana lord made a sour face but did not complain since he saw Baron "Flekte" was not displeased that he was angry. He just kept on questioning:

"Did you go to school any?"

"With the Jesuit fathers in Ljubljana," answered Jurij, "and even then they told us how a learned Jesuit had written a thick book in which he proved that witches simply don't exist."

"What, a Jesuit? Who is that father?" yelled Frueberger. "Have his name written down so that he doesn't escape just punishment!"

Provost Urh recalled that the most illustrious bishop Joannes Franciscus knew of that Jesuit. He gave the name of some German count, but the name did not remain in my memory, thus I cannot write it down here.

"Count…?" Frueberger curled right up. "A German count, you say, lord provost? Well, then everything is all right, we won't write anything down!" He was simply dying from excess humility, for that man only showed courage to those beneath him, but to those above him he was ever a humble sheep!

They called Marks Wulffing to testify. We sensed that his testimony would be important and that it would probably decide life or death. He walked with a stick and showed how his leg was still hurting. He genuflected and beat his breast before the judges as was his custom. The lord magistrate was pleased with that: he was especially nice to the witness. He reminded him to tell everything and not to fear, since the court had so much power that it would take any witness under its protection if his testimony were just and true.

And, indeed, Marks Wulffing recalled everything. He recounted quite clearly that one night when the moon was shining he was lying in the barn, and he could not fall asleep because all the while it seemed to him that something was humming or rumbling in the air. He got up and looked at the sky through the little round window in the hayloft. Soon he noticed there above him four spots in the sky, and those spots were rumbling. They then came down towards the Visoko roof, and they played with each other like swallows, after which three flew off, but one came down in the yard by the

200

house. There she jumped off the pig, which sped right into the pigshed. Her he recognized clearly: for certain it was Agata Schwarzkobler—had he not recognized her by anything else, he would certainly have recognized her golden hair.

When the sewing bee broke up at Debelak's, Agata struck him with her hand. With that slap he suddenly felt a fire kindled in his left leg, right in the calf. From then on there was a live coal in that leg and he suffered torment as if someone had encircled his shin with a white-hot piece of iron. It burned and scorched him, but his leg did not swell up, which appeared to him to be something truly strange, since it is after all impossible for flesh not to swell when pain infests it. About all of this he told no one, because no one would have begun to believe he was hurting if nothing showed.

However, one Sunday night the pains were too terrible. He got up and cut deep into his calf with a sharp knife. Out from the cut fell an angular piece of flint, two needles and two pointy nails, which he had already presented to the lords. Not very much blood flowed, which again seemed strange to him.

The Ljubljana assessor took a small basket into his hands and removed from it packet after packet. He said: "Here is the flint, here are the two needles, here are the two nails; everything is covered with human blood, which is surely proof that Marks Wulffing spoke the truth."

Urša Prekova did not second him. She turned to Neža Bergant and asked loudly: "Neža, have you ever seen a man that could lie like that bum of Jeremija's lied?"

Urša answered: "Nowhere, never!"

201

Marks was not put off. He bent down, undid the wrappings on his left foot, bared his calf and showed the bright scar, saying: "Here was the wound."

The sight of that wound strongly affected the judges; therefore they asked Agata if she had anything to add to Marks's testimony. But she only answered that it was not true.

The withered man from Ljubljana became angry: "When she's on the pyre she'll still be saying it's not true!"

Magistrate Mändl spoke up: "So, we're at the end of the testimony! It went more quickly than I thought. What now?"

Once again, the first to have a say was old Frueberger, who thrust himself to the center of things and acted as if he was important. He made me sick, like a mangy dog that jumps at people.

"It is absolutely clear that now comes the questioning with torture, because otherwise you can't say this was a respectable inquest!"—that is what that Frueberger growled. "If we hasten a bit and if our helper behind us here," the old man looked over at the frajman, "carries out his work as he ought, we can still finish everything today in God's name."

"She seems a bit weak to me," worried the black one from Ljubljana, "she could not endure an examination by torment for long. But I agree that without such examination it's not an inquest. Maybe just give a directive that we delay everything until tomorrow so the sinner can gain a bit of strength overnight?"

Lord Frueberger was extremely displeased. "Why should we lose this whole afternoon? That won't do!

What are we doing as assessors? If we don't want to light a little fire under the accused today to warm her limbs, we still have other aids that will have to be used. It is really a difficult case, as always when the devil is involved. Even if in God's name the examination by torment is put off until tomorrow, we cannot do nothing this afternoon, since after all we are responsible judges! If I had it my way, we would do some test, let's say with the sewing needle. It is my conviction that we cannot do without the needle," he bleated like a hoarse ram. "'Nadelprob,' 'nadelprob,'" the disgusting old man wailed a couple of times and his eyes strained to his forehead.

"What's that?" asked the younger Frueberger's wife, Rozala, of Mihol Schwaiffstrigkh, who was in the crowd, leaning on the fence right next to her.

Mihol Schwaiffstrigkh answered importantly: "The thing is, they undress her, they take off all her clothes— ah, why should I hide it from you—they strip her naked. Because every person has marks on their body, they will poke a needle in those marks to see whether or not there is any blood in her."

The womenfolk stiffened and it would surely have led to an outburst had not the lord magistrate begun to speak. He for one stated the opinion that the needle test did not belong in a public place, nor would it do to allow children and young men in.

"Let's go to the castle," suggested Frueberger, "there we'll get a suitable place."

They probably would have quarreled some more, because it seemed to me that the black one from Ljubljana was also preparing to snarl something, but Provost Urh Falenič approached the judges from his seat. In his hands he carried a large, thick letter with a seal. He put the letter on the table, saying: "From the most illustrious and high lord bishop."

The magistrate and assessors instantly stood up, took off their hats, and put them in front of themselves. When the letter was unsealed, the chairman read it. Today I can no longer say what was written beneath the heavy seal, because almost twenty years have passed since then. I do still recall that the bishop decreed and made it known to everyone that he had reviewed everything in the case of Agata Ema Schwarzkobler—what was taken down and heard—and that he was convinced that no proof would be found to ascertain the truth beyond all doubt. Finally, Joannes Franciscus decreed, and notified everyone who would hear, that the accused should be tested by water, and in such a manner that she would be cleansed should she come out of the water alive by any means. He designated nine o'clock the next morning as the hour for the holy inquest, and on that spot below Škofja Loka where the two Sora rivers flow into one another.

With that the day's trial had reached an end, the magistrate ordered that the accused be led away to confinement in the town hall, that the heavy chains be taken off her, and that she be locked up there all night until she would be led to the place where the water would prove her innocence or her wickedness! At the same time, since it was possible that this night would be the last in Agata Ema Schwarzkobler's life, the community was directed to provide everything she might wish for and name. Several aged women could also be let in to stay the night with her and pray, if she had the desire now and then to pray.

Now it once again happened that my brother Jurij aroused general interest and—I can also write—general satisfaction. I was on my bench and did not go to her to acknowledge her as mine before the whole world; worldly pride still tormented me. But my brother Jurij leapt forward again, took her in his arms, and carried her from the stage to the little wagon, so that the irons jangled and the women were immediately crying out loud. Agata had suffered much the whole morning, suffered torments that the most fiendish one of all could not think up. So it is not surprising that, the instant Jurij took her from the stage, she relinquished her final strength and collapsed unconscious into his arms.

He did not consider for long: he jumped into the wagon with her, sat right next to her, and grasped her around the waist with a strong arm so she could not fall from her seat. Her head fell onto his shoulder, and he called out confidently: "Drive, Schwaiffstrigkh!" And Mihol started the little horse as if there a man that justice had no power over was sitting in the wagon. Two halberdiers marched on either side of the wagon, and the people thanked Jurij loudly. No one talked about me.

The Loka womenfolk would not settle down that afternoon. The greatest anger was whipped up against Marks Wulffing, who, in the womenfolk's united opinion, gave false evidence. The butcher's wife, the baker's wife, Mother Bergant, her maid, and servants searched the whole city for the false witness. Around five o'clock they tracked Marks down in Oslovska Street, as he was going into Bergant's. He had not yet gotten properly seated when Oslovska Street was already teeming with agitated women, old and young.

Bergant, a shrewd chap, acted as circumstances dictated: he called on Marks to leave the tavern because he would not get a drink from him. Marks felt the shame of that summons, immediately got up and in his recklessness stepped into Oslovska Street. The hags let out a shriek and rushed at him. Since he was extremely strong, at first he fended them off, pushed them aside and thus forced his way onto the square. But there he met ever more enemies. The first had come empty-handed, but the later ones were carrying brooms in their hands. They said absolutely nothing, just swung at him, and Marks Wulffing soon realized that he could not stay around much longer. He bore several more blows and then took off running for the Water Gate. But the women were after him like a pack of hunting dogs after a rabbit raised from the heather on a hill-crest. He did not even dare look back. He raced across the bridge and past the Capuchin church where the masons were working. When the women passed by chasing Wulffing's son, the masons immediately realized what was happening. Mortar and lime flew at the escapee so that Marks looked like a wall that had been freshly plastered.

And so Marks Wulffing's testimony ended ingloriously! He disappeared from that day, not even his own people knew where to.

That afternoon, it went badly for someone else as well. As soon as the bishop's letter was read, Rozalija and Frueberger hurried home by the quickest path. But the judges, behind whom I too was walking, slowly trod to the square with the crowd and there took leave of each other right in front of Frueberger's house. The old noble Frueberger said good-bye to everyone and it was quite obvious by looking at him that he was pleased with himself and the honor done him as an assessor. Not suspecting anything wrong, he stepped into the entryway of his house.

"Just look," his own wife greeted him, "you came home anyway? I thought for sure that you took off with some Jane."

"What's wrong?" he asked innocently.

But the old woman did not have time to answer because young Rozalija appeared on the field of battle. "You don't know, mother—I just didn't dare look anywhere, I was so ashamed! Think, our father wanted her to be undressed and he wanted to examine her entire naked body."

She began crying hard. But the older woman wasn't crying; she measured her husband with such a poisonous look that old Frueberger very quickly slipped into a side room.

Thus, that day, God punished our Agata's the two worst enemies.

XIII.

Once again I write that Škofja Loka never saw such days as when they tried Agata Schwarz-kobler. The oldest people, who had often watched as Gavžnik took the life of a poor sinner, swore that never had such crowds besieged the town. There was not room for everyone in the houses, even though as many of them as possible were put up in taverns and with acquaintances. The square was just swarming with people who did not have lodging. The beer cellars immediately jacked up their prices, the butchers were continually slaughtering cattle and killing smaller animals, causing one to think that he had strayed into the camp of a large army, for which ample provisions had to be prepared. Despite all of this, no one wanted to go home, and our servant cursed especially hard when he had to go back to Visoko with the two horses, since Jurij and I did not know how many days we would have to stay in Loka. But the folk knew how to look after themselves: they settled down in the grain fields and hay and spent the night under a fine sky. When darkness fell on the valley, there were so many fires burning around Puštal and around Kamnitnik that you could not count them. Clever merchants infested the swarms and sold every trifle dearly. Many among the crowd were placated by the fact that tomorrow the water would not mar the fun and that she would probably be burned, or at least they would cut off her head. Many of them could have fallen asleep in that hope! Such is man: each has a corner in his heart from which flows some pleasant malice when a fellow human falls into misfortune! There was eating and there was drinking, and if the pots were emptied, they were heaped full and put on the fire again!

Agata was locked in the town hall. Neither the butcher nor baker's wives, neither Mother Bergant, nor the other goodies who firmly believed in the girl's innocence, left her. They fired, they baked, and they even heated sweet wine for her, so that Agata sat as if at a wedding table. But she could not eat much. She sampled the food but little and she cried a lot; at long last she fell asleep and slept until early morning, just as if she expected a happy day, and not a cold death in the water, or even a hot death on the pyre.

About ten o'clock, and even before, the public again began to press into the town and the square was teeming with curiosity seekers like the day before. Then Lord Joannes Franciscus arrived from the castle. Over the red trimmed robe he had put on a white surplice, on his head he wore a reddish cap, and he had a wide stole around his neck. Immediately news spread that the most illustrious lord bishop himself wanted to hear Agata Schwarzkobler's confession. The bishop himself wanted to prepare our Agata for the next world and cleanse her soul of its sins, if she had any. Never had anyone in Škofja Loka partaken of such an honor, and Fuehrnpfeill himself later told me that even in the oldest records, of which there are plenty in the castle, you cannot read of an occasion when the Freising bishop ever administered the sacrament of Holy Penance to a Loka subject.

He heard her confession a long time. What they spoke of I do not know; no one knew anything about it, which is understandable. Neither has Agata breathed a wit of it to me as long as I have lived, and I have not dared to inquire, knowing well that she would not tell me anything.

At ten the large bell at St. Jakob's sang out. It sang briefly and it sang sadly, the way a funeral bell sings. In a flash the square was on its knees, and I saw old men wiping their eyes. Provost Urh slowly stepped between the kneeling, and he carried God in his arms, raising him and blessing with Him those who were praying. Again, I write that there had never been such a Communion on the Loka square, and there surely will never be one like it as long as our beautiful and rich town, which is the most beautiful our Carniolan lands number, stands—only Ljubljana is possibly more beautiful.

When Communion was finished, the town guard emptied the square and the public had to move off. They hurried to the water and once more covered all the banks and Puštal meadows, and even on the other side of the Selščica it was head to head. The lord bishop sternly commanded that the children stay home, but I nevertheless saw them later as they crowded to the windows and pressed their little heads against the glass to sate their curiosity.

At half past ten, the bell at St. Jakob's sang out again and my sorrowful soul sensed that the bell's voice was truly the voice of a real funereal bell! On the square, the procession, the likes of which the inhabitants had never seen, formed ranks. In front walked the fraternity of Corpus Christi and behind them yet other fraternities, but they did not carry banners with them because it would not due to have a banner waving in the air when a person is being accompanied on his last trip. Next marched the Loka burghers and their wives, and I can say that only the oldest remained at home.

Towards the end came Agata—though so many years have passed, I still see her today as she stepped from the town jail into the bright day. She wore no clothing but a long white shirt reaching down to her feet, which in places clung to the maidenly limbs of her maidenly body. She resembled a heavenly angel, especially because her unbraided golden hair fell upon her thin figure. When she took a step we saw how her foot shook, and when the breeze played with her shirt—my God—black blotches could also be seen on her white legs where the heavy iron chains had rubbed.

But each time she bowed modestly to prevent the white dress from being raised. Jesus and Mary! Perhaps she was walking the path that led to her death after all, and on a most beautiful day, when there was not the smallest cloud in God's sky and when the sun was shining as if it meant to laugh at her who had suffered so much!

The lord provost marched at her side, but did not speak to her—and what would he have said, when she had been so nicely reconciled with her God, who was the master of her life! In the middle of the road, when we had already turned down the slope below the Poljane Gate, Father Falenič began to pray the holy litany for the dying, because that is what Lord Joannes Franciscus had ordered. He began: "Kyrie eleison!—Christ, have mercy!" The exclamations that were particularly appropriate to the state of our poor Agata he repeated three times, so that he sighed three times each: "Who prolonged the life of the mortally ill King Ezekiel!—Who took the fever from the king's son when he lay dying!—Who brought the widow's dead son back to life and restored him to her!—Who called the centurion's daughter back to life!"

Each time he answered himself: "Lord, have mercy!"—and then the crowd shouted after him: "Have mercy!" This calling rose to the throne whereon was seated our Lord Jesus Christ, who later judged her rightly and prolonged her life, as he prolonged it for the dead daughter of the centurion!

Overnight they had also moved the fences. Today a smaller area was fenced precisely where the gravel forms a fairly long and initially wide tongue between the two streams that flow into one another there. Once more there was a table for the judge and his assessors. Everyone was already at their places. Joannes Franciscus himself sat on a special chair, and today he wore over his shoulders a thick gold chain and on it a cross that sparkled with precious stones. Permission had also been granted Jurij and me to cross the fence. Below by the water there were some more castle servants, among them in a boat was the huntmaster, who was the castle fisherman as well. All the rest of the crowd had to stay outside the fence. And opposite, on the Puštal bank, were gathered the Loka goodies, about whom I have written so much.

They stopped with Agata on the spot where she had to step into the water, into the Poljanščica, she was from the Poljane Valley.

Since the litany had not yet been completely prayed, Lord Urh continued: "By Your tears and with Your sorrow!—By Your dread and with Your bloody sweat!—By Your holy wounds, by Your cross and suffering!" The crowds shouted: "Save her, oh Lord!" and that call, multiplied from rank to rank, eventually spread like thunder over the mountains. "On the day of judgment!" Once again there thundered: "We beseech You, save us, oh Lord!" Only Bishop Janez Frančišek sat on his chair as if cut from stone.

At St. Jakob's it struck eleven times. The bell once again boomed out from the loopholes high up. The litanies were at an end. All of the noise died down.

The bishop signaled with his white hand. The provost stepped up to Agata and spoke with her about something. Then the bitter and painful hour was due to begin. Holy Trinity, be our savior!

At first Agata looked back at the lord provost as he was walking away from her. He had certainly told her that her time had now come. At that she looked over the water up our valley. She looked in that direction quite a while, and we could see how her breast moved with her deep breathing. Gradually she turned around. Today, too, her eye rested on the gray mountain slopes where the peaks were as white as her face, in which there was not even a drop of blood. Then she looked before herself into the water. There in front of her there was a shoal, but further down the surface was darkish green, as always where it is deep. The water there was also whirling and turning the dirty froth about.

Agata crossed herself, bent down, pressed the shirt around her legs, and bravely stepped into the water. There was fine sand near the edge and it was easy to walk. But then the shale began and she was cut as she stepped on it. It was already up over her knees, so that her rounded limbs showed and some of her hair was already floating on the surface.

The onlookers held their breath. Then the butcher's wife shouted out: "Turn back, poor dear, you're already in the water! Turn back and you'll come onto dry land alive!"

Since Agata did not respond to the shout, the butcher's wife went into a rage: "After all you're not deaf!"

And others too shouted: "Turn around!"

Any person would have been confused in that situation, and so it was with Agata—that yelling surely threw her into even greater confusion. She pressed on, entered the stream, and the water roared about her and very quickly toppled her. All at once the maiden was in the waves, but she got up again, the scant clothing had clung tightly to her limbs, and she stood before her judges as if without any clothes.

The crowds stood stock still and not a voice was heard from the black droves. At that moment a miracle occurred—I cannot write any differently.

Right by the water, an ash was growing, and it must have been very old for its top showed dry branches. With all the noise, with such a great gathering of people, a young flycatcher had sat on a dry branch. It was not afraid of the shouting or the crowds. "Ček!" it went and flew down from the ash. It chased around Agata's head for the small flies that were swarming in the air. Two swallows also chased down along the Poljanščica and danced around the girl a few times, who we were now almost certain would not come out of the water alive. That was later talked about for years and years. The Loka womenfolk fell to their knees and the holy Our Father prayer resounded loudly. But I was not stirred by any of this, and something in my soul kept saying: "Perhaps she is guilty after all."

Now Agata was trying to wade ahead. And she actually managed a couple of steps into the stream, but it was apparent that she would not withstand the water. Then I had occasion to notice clearly how the bishop Joannes Franciscus raised his hand and made a sign. At that sign the castle huntsman, who was also the castle fisherman, deftly shoved off from the edge in the little boat and turned it toward the deep water. Meanwhile, the power of the waives toppled Agata and she quickly disappeared below the surface. The people shouted, and with all his might the huntsman rowed to the place where the girl had gone under. Schwaiffstrigkh and his guard shouted: "Quiet, people, quiet!"

So it was at that moment that I stood on the bank, just as if I had a heavy iron on each leg, and I could not even move from the place. And at that moment it also happened that my brother Jurij jumped into the water with his clothes and shoes on. Around him the water burled and splashed high, so that I, being in the area, came under a shower and was wetted almost just as much as he, who was already swimming through the waters. He lunged a few times and he was at her side as she again appeared in the middle of the deep water. He wrapped a strong arm around her and, with the other, made powerful circles, so that they were very soon at a place where the water was shallow.

There, he put the girl on the soft sand and said: "And now, Agata, I ask you in God's name, walk, so that you come out of the water alive!"

Whether or not Agata understood him, I do not know. Yet she took a few steps, but she did not take many, because the Loka womenfolk poured down to her from the gravel bank; while still in the water, they surrounded her with their bodies and hid her from the onlookers, so that the uninvited eye could not look upon her soaked, poorly clad figure. They took her from the water in front of the judges and quite simply carried her from the unhappy spot. They also called to Jurij that he had to come with them because he was soaked and needed to change. Wherever they passed, the people moved out of the way, until they carried her to Wohlgemuet's, where the lady of the house did not give in until they put Agata in the wide, soft marriage bed of Wohlgemuet's mother.

Mother Bergant could not contain herself at these sights. She stood in the shallow water, and, when her companions had carried the girl away, she raised her fist at the judges and shouted with all her might: "You won't look at her anymore, you old sinners! And you, moldy Frueberger, if it's to sew human bodies with needles that you want, darn your own! You good for nothing!"

Laughter burst out all around and even JoannesFranciscus on his red chair spread his lips a little. That is how the Loka wives and maids behaved on that occasion!

I have this to write: Centuries and centuries may pass, but may the Loka womenfolk keep the spirit that they had in them in the year of our Lord 1695, when that spirit was as bright as gold and as pure as the sun's rays! May heaven hear me!*

Some onlookers had gone after Agata, since there was no longer anything special to be expected now that she had come out of the water alive. However, a great deal still awaited them, for the bishop and judges continued to sit calmly, and they were the ones who had to pronounce judgment.

The bishop had already sent the provost to the judges, who were conferring about something among themselves, when Schwaiffstrigkh stepped up and said that a woman was at the fence demanding with all her might that the judges hear her. Lord "Flekte" would not be swayed, saying that there had already been more than enough witnesses as it was.

"She's having a fit and crying and cannot be sent away," assured Schwaiffstrigkh.

The bishop uttered something in Latin, at which the magistrate ordered the woman to present herself before

* That plea was heard!

him and the judges. When she arrived, it was Margareta Wulffing. It was apparent from looking at her that she had made a long journey, for her clothes were in disarray and her face was all worn.

She started right in: "We only heard yesterday that you in Loka meant to burn Izidor's betrothed and that our Marks testified against her. I walked all night and I prayed the whole way. Not that! A person isn't an animal and you don't burn wood under him! Not that!"

Janez Frančišek calmed her: "Don't hurry so, lass! Tell us who you are and where you come from!"

In her confusion she did not recognized the lord bishop. She answered: "I wish to speak with those who sit in judgment and who want to take the life of Izidor's betrothed…"

"Who are you and what do you want?" the bishop replied somewhat more sharply, for he did not like to put up with contradictions.

"Watch it, eh. Think, eh. You're speaking with our most high lord bishop!" Schwaiffstrigkh put in. "It's Marks Wulffing's sister, your mercy!"

"Speak!" ordered Joannes Franciscus curtly and sharply.

Margareta told how last year around Ascension she came upon her brother Marks in the little room in the attic. He was alone and thought that no one saw him, but she was watching him from the small window in the loft. And she watched how he cut deeply into the calf on his leg with a sharp knife, so that a lot of blood flowed out. In that blood he wetted a sharp-edged stone, two nails and a few needles. He bound the wound and after

219

that he went about like a cripple for several weeks, but did not tell anyone what was the matter with him.

When the magistrate showed her the bloody flint, the nails, and needles, she answered that all of it was what Marks had wetted in his own blood.

The bishop broke his silence: "Have all of this written down!"

First those who were standing at the fence told others standing farther back that Marks Wulffing had testified falsely and had wetted the nails and needles in his blood himself. That story spread from row to row and soon it was blaring over the Puštal meadows as well as under Kamnitnik: "Marks Wulffing was not telling the truth!" They cursed the false witness, and it was truly fortunate that Marks had hauled his bones off the day before, because that day the crowd would have ripped him apart.

Margareta's testimony was written down in its entirety, and the court declared aloud that there was no fault with Agata Ema Schwarzkobler.

At that moment, Joannes Franciscus indicated to the lord magistrate that he would like to speak before the gathering. The guard hurried among the people and, when it was learned that the bishop himself wanted to speak, they pressed to the banks, and it was a miracle that a few did not fall into the water. The public was also pressing against the fence.

Janez Frančišek stood up from his seat and had his Mass attire brought; the provost put his high bishop's hat on his head and handed him his heavy pastor's staff.

He began to speak and in such a voice that I did not know from where in his frail body he drew it. He said that he did not raise his eyes those two days, he was so ashamed of the judges and of us, who had come to gloat over the bloody death of a young maiden. He added: "You were as many as the leaves and grass and you even dragged your children with you just to see the ruin of a young girl who had done no harm to any of you. You were not Christians, you were beasts who thirsted after the blood of an innocent and for this you will bear a heavy responsibility at the hour of your death!"

The ranks were falling to their knees and the women's crying was heard. And he also told us that God does not know witches and that it is a mortal affront to God if someone, whoever it may be, affirms that it is possible for our God to hand a child over to the devil at birth.

I was noticing with great satisfaction how the black judge from Ljubljana hung his hooked nose and how Lord Frueberger looked straight ahead somewhat stupidly, like a young ox that the butcher had hit over the head too lightly.

Further the bishop said that Agata Schwarzkobler had taken on a great sacrifice for all of us, and that, with her suffering, she had cleansed our souls and lit a lamp in the darkness in which those souls groped. "May God forgive us the sin we committed against that woman, especially the judges and also you who yearned for the blood of an innocent person." And he solemnly promised that as long as he would have authority over executions at Loka castle he would not allow anyone else to be prosecuted for witchcraft.

"That is what I wanted to tell you," he concluded. "You, lord provost, I ask to tell the people in their own words in case anyone has not understood me."

Lord Urh explained even more harshly in our own native language what dumb heifers and bull-calves we had been when we believed that Agata Schwarzkobler had caused hail and ridden through the sky on a pig, and that the lord bishop said that there was no greater stupidity than the stupid belief in black magic.

The crowds were repentant and everyone carried the bishop Janez Frančišek in his heart, and he seemed like an apostle to us as he trod from the trial towards the church, giving his pastoral blessing.

Thus ended the test by water and Agata Schwarzkobler emerged from it cleansed! God be praised and thanked that he preordained it all to a just end and did not take a young life that certainly would not have wanted to leave the green earth on which we all depend!

Although we were more in need of rest than any other day of the year, my brother and I did not get to sleep that night. Acquaintances and friends, who spoke of their joy that everything had ended so happily, arrived first. I did not even know that I had so many friends in Loka! They also drank wine on my account, which could not be prevented since I continued to be the master of two holdings. Even the lord notary of the castle came to celebrate with me. To commemorate the celebration, he brought a letter about the quartered Finkenstein, which I had asked him for many times and which until now he did not want to give me.

Thus it was that famous letter entered the Visoko records.

At around eleven o'clock, Agata woke from a deep sleep. But, lo, relief had not come over her in her sleep!

Her face burned and she could not stop crying. She wanted out of the town, she wanted to go home at all cost. Only to Visoko, and in the deepest darkness, so that the world could not see her as she returned to the place the castle servants had driven her from! Jurij and I had to give in to her for she would have gone mad, the way she was behaving. We borrowed a horse and it was long past midnight when we left the town. I sat in the saddle and took her in front of me. And Jurij led the horse on foot so we could go forward in the dark.

In the cool of night she calmed down a bit and quieted her sighing and sobbing. We were already riding towards Schefferten, and then she leaned into my arms. Heat wafted from her like from an oven, and I had almost nothing to hold in my arms!

First there were a few muffled words, just as if she were talking to someone else and not to me. Then she sobbed: "Izidor, if it would have been done your way, I would have had to go to the pyre! You, too, oh Jesus! believed everything that Marks Wulffing said and…" Very quietly she added, "by the Seven Sorrows of our Beloved Mother! I know well that some will even believe those lies in years to come!"

I did not answer her. "And I loved you so much," she sighed,"more a sister cannot love a brother!"And after a while:

"It's hard for Jurij to walk. Izidor, let him on the horse a little." Immediately I got down. At that moment, as I slid to the ground, I noticed that the chains had also left their marks on her arms. The moon shone from behind the Stanišče Mountains and the valley was shining in its beams.

"I won't even dare go to church," cried Agata and put her hands in her clothing to hide the reminders of jail from me.

She and Jurij climbed into the saddle, and I took the tether in my hand. We did not talk the while, and Why? when it was right that not just one was on the horse the whole way. We went on through the valley and the water rushed powerfully on our left.

The girl rested on Jurij. They whispered something between themselves, then something else again, and suddenly Agata embraced him about his neck. It was not long before she fell asleep and so the whispering up there in the saddle stopped too.

When I looked back at the two of them something in me snapped and a veil fell so that I could see everything that was behind it. And then my soul came between two heavy millstones that spun more and more quickly, and that soul shook and twisted in great suffering! My worldly arrogance was crushed, and the little pedestal on which it stood was crushed with it! In that torment I could hear, as if a voice coming from heaven: "Izidor, she is innocent, at Loka you were condemned! You lost the maiden that was destined for you!"

I paced on and on by the horse, but I would happily have fallen to the ground and pulled the hair from my head. It was plain to me that she had chosen another, and I was fully aware of my oath that I could not prevent her from that!

Then divine mercy came upon me and filled me with the knowledge that no wrong was being done to me: God denied me the bride that I myself had denied before—in order that a shadow would not be cast on the two Visoko holdings!

When the millstones stopped and when my exhausted soul got a little strength, I knew that I must do penance not only for my poor father, but even more so for myself, for my great sins.

Towards morning we crossed the ford at Visoko—I was still so distraught that I did not feel the cold water as I stepped through it—but Agata kept on sleeping. And I at the moment was no longer the master of the two holdings that lay before me in the morning dimness and that were so famous through the whole Poljane Valley—I was no longer master of the land Polikarp Khallan had left me, that after my oversight they would be deserving of an even better name, and that Agata's children might wash from it the sinful and mercilessly spilt blood and bring down on it a new blessing from heaven! But I was not worthy of that blessing because my worldly arrogance was greater than the love that I should have had for my betrothed. My hand had given offense, for that I had to reach for the axe and cut it off at a blow, so that what was unhealthy on me would fall from me!

Always do thus, sinner, so that your soul be cured!

XIV.

Agata took to her bed and she stayed there a full month; we were afraid for her life. As for me, I did not stray a step from the path I had walked that night when leading the horse from Schefferten to Visoko.

As soon as Agata got up, I disclosed to her and Jurij that I was handing over both holdings to the two of them and that I was joining the army. Just at that time the estates of the realm had ordered a large military call-up among the country folk. My God, were there tears and love! But they refused, saying they did not want to have Visoko. I did not relent. In Loka, at the castle, we did everything as was proper lest any misunderstandings or quarrels arise in the future I retained for myself half of the upper house so I might have my own corner should someday I return, and maybe even with a ball in my body. I held to the division of money, too—so much as was allotted to my brother Jurij.

We held a wedding the like of which there had been few in the valley. Then I set off. I carried only as much as I needed to get to Ljubljana, and after that became an expense of the emperor, who was quite happy to take me into his army.

I quickly took leave of Agata and Jurij. I looked at the colorful church of Saint Volnik one more time and turned my face up the valley with its green forests, and after all that, I went off with a small bag over my shoulder, and even that was almost empty. Thus the once rich Visokan left his farm: but he did not carry a tempest within; all was peaceful in him and he knew that it was God's will, all of it, and that all of it was a part of his penance!

Let me note right here that it was in the year 1695 and that I did not return until the spring of the year of our Lord 1707.

Be it also related in this place how they lived at Visoko during those years. I write what was told to me about it, but everything is true and reliable.

Jurij and Agata lived as married people ought and are commanded to do: the master and lady did not know conflict and were like wheels on a wagon that are always pulled along the same track. With the passing of time, Agata once again regained her strength but she no longer had her previous joyfulness. There were always a few clouds over her face that remained from the time she was tried at Loka. That judgment she continued to drag with her on a heavy chain about her leg, an even heavier iron was attached to the chain than criminals have on the Venetian Republic's galleys. The world is foolish and evil!

First it began with the Debelaks. The old master had left his farm to his son Peter. And soon after the transfer, he died. The son was scarcely like his father. He was quarrelsome and he had an angry remark on his tongue at the least excuse. Jurij and Peter had words on account of the boundary, the lot of which was worth less than the wool from a sheep that has already been shorn. One word led to another. And when Agata intruded into it for no reason, Peter replied to her thus: "You be quiet! Thank God that you weren't burned alive at Loka! Had not the bishop helped you—God knows what you gave him?—they surely would have hoisted you on the stake!"

At that, the venomous man even roared with laughter so that he almost choked. Agata sat down in the grass, and Jurij howled like a wounded soldier doesas the surgeons are sawing off an arm. The servant and he grabbed poles, knocked Debelak to the ground, and beat him, so that he spent long months groaning in bed. He made a complaint at the castle. When the matter had been investigated, Joannes Franciscus came to Loka once again. The magistrate presented him the documents, and the lord bishop looked them over from beginning to end. Great was his anger and his arm struck terribly! He ordered that Jurij and the servant not be harmed.

But he sent Peter Debelak to the castle prison, where he sat more than a whole year. One afternoon a band of castle halberdiers rode up to Visoko. With them came the castle magistrate and, what caused everyone to wonder, the bishop Janez Frančišek himself came. He came to visit our Agata and honor her before all of the people of Poljane! Since there were wines in the cellar—being that Jurij too traded in the Vipava country—they could give him a drink; what they gave him to eat I do not know. The gracious lord stayed at Visoko a whole hour. When he was leaving, he gave Agata a picture of himself that master Remp had done on canvas, so that you could look at him as if he were alive in front of you. The picture was in a gold frame. Even today we are proud to have Janez Frančišek in the upper house and we show him to everyone that comes to visit us at Visoko.[*]

Thus the Loka bishop honored Agata Schwarzkobler, now Khallan by marriage, to the shame of all the evil tongues! And the feud with the Debelaks kept on—on account of a worthless and overgrown piece of turf that Jurij and Peter could have renounced at no loss. And even now, when I, Izidor Khallan, have returned to beneath my father's roof, that feud has not ceased. While harsh words are not exchanged, still one house does not look at the other. When will things ever improve in this world?

I was away from home for almost eleven years and I served in armies that Lord Prince Eugenius commanded. It was a hard living for me and there were almost always more cudgels than rations. But I never forgot my God or my native land, which I thought of even in the worst heat of bloody engagements and likewise when we were idle in winter quarters. No one who has not been in a war himself knows what war is! The ordinary folk are always and everywhere battered when armies fight: no life is safe then, neither woman nor child is safe. All such things I saw with my own eyes: I saw death carry off old men, I saw violence done to girls, I saw huts

[*] It is still at Visoko today.

burned, cities pillaged and leveled. My heart was not in that bloody handiwork; St. Izidor be my witness that I did not take part in massacres or pillaging!

I remained true to my service because I had sworn to, and there was no force that would have made me disloyal to the regiment's standard. Nonetheless, I did not enjoy war and I prayed to God that he would halt it with his powerful arm. But the truth is that I endured a lot of war, which at that time raged around us, so that we never caught our breath.

What I write now, be it recorded for the purpose that those who will live at Visoko after us may know that great misfortune came upon their ancestors, who did not live in such good times as those in which they would live!

First, we were at Zenta, where we took a Turkish camp, killed thirty thousand Turks, and even slew the chief vizier, leaving the Turkish sultan to weep quite basely for him. There was booty to spare and I too was allotted a just share. Later we raged into Italy, and Prince Eugenius drove the French before him. At Cremona we took a French general, and at Luzzara Lord Eugenius pummeled them again. Later they took us from Italy and moved us to Germany, again against the French. At Hochstatt we had a bloody battle because the English were also with us. Nice people, strong men, but they speak a language that they probably barely understand themselves! When they were throwing me here and there I got used to Italian and French, but not to English! At Hochstatt Eugenius overcame them on the left flank after heavy losses, because the Parci, who at that time were siding with the French, resisted mightily. There I saw the French general who has a name like a priest's robe.[*]

Up to that time I remained healthy through all the engagements. Bullets whistled by me, Turkish sabers glinted above me, they cut at me with backswords and thrust halberds at me, but God our Father watched over me, and my body remained unharmed. My soul I protected by myself, lest it come to harm. My behavior was pleasing to those who were placed above me, and therefore after a long and arduous service I achieved the considerable honor of being named a corporal. I was also in the glorious battle at Turin, where our valiant captain, lord Daun, was in the clutches of the French. We hurried to help him and jumped the high French ramparts. Our small enemies shot at us from wherever they could, and many of ours rolled down the sand bank, mortally wounded.

I was almost to the top, and at that point there were some imperials who wanted to run away down the hill. I beat them with a cudgel and drove them on. Then it seemed to me that one of those cowards stabbed me in the chest. Without expecting it at all, I was lying on the ground, and on my left side, above the heart, blood was quickly spreading over my clothes. I was struck, not by a rebellious hand, but by a French musket! What happened then I do not remember.

When I regained consciousness, I was lying in the ambulatory. I was bandaged and could not move my

[*] Marshal Talard.

limbs. I lay on boards and could not feel the bones within me. And yet it seemed to me that all was light inside, that I was resting on soft clouds and that I was swaying with them across the sky! When I looked about the space around me, there were quite a few lying on the same kind of beds. All were bandaged and the blood rose to the light of day in red lines. But, wait, then it was I noticed that my chest was bandaged; and when I turned my head to the left, I saw that my bandages too were heavily bloodied. Then I recalled that I had fallen in battle and that I was shot, just the way that the gypsy woman on Blegoš had foretold.

At that moment it happened that a small man of whom there was nothing of note entered the ambulatory. Upon entering he took his three-cornered hat from his head with great respect. After him followed a whole slew of nothing but generals and officers on whom a great deal of gold shone and whose clothes were embroidered with fine, expensive needlework. Prince Eugenius, however, did not wear gold or overly much embroidery, but, despite that, one could recognize right away that he was our general. He walked up to each bed, conversed with the lowest solder and comforted him on his bed of pain and suffering. If the medics told him quietly that the wounds were mortal and would soon surely take the patient's life, he placed his hand on the wounded man's forehead and said, "Merci bien!" which in our language means that Lord Prince Eugenius was thanking him for the labor he had sacrificed.

He came to me, too, but I could not answer because of my great weakness. The medics whispered something, at which the general placed his tiny and soft hand on my hot forehead, saying "Merci bien!"—that was the only thanks that was given me for having dragged my body for hire into the Italian lands on behalf of the emperor, who later did not ask after me at all, or about how it went with me and how I was getting along!

The next morning, I awoke, and behold, next to me yesterday's empty bed had received a patient: at night they had brought in a heavy cavalryman who was now lying there. They had cut off a hand and a leg, so that he was in wide bandages. He was so weak that he did not utter a sound, no matter how unbearable his pains were.

And so I awoke and turned my eyes unwillingly to the neighboring bed. Before me lay a man with a long, thin face covered with a wild beard and in which the eyes were set in deep pits, just as on a corpse. I kept my gaze fixed upon this neighbor and the thought forced itself into my weak brain: *Where had I seen the man before?* Thus I looked upon him for hours. At last, my neighbor awoke as well, and in the pits on his face two small dim lights were fading. He moaned badly and then turned his gaze to me and we looked each other in the eye for hours on end.

My God! Where had I seen that face before? It was furrowed and barren like a field that has been hit by a torrential downpour! Neither of us could move and we could not even raise our heads, only look at one another. At last, as if from a distance, a weary voice sounded from way over a hill: "Izidor—it is surely you, Izidor?"

Mother of God!—It was in truth Marks Wulffing, abandoned and cast off by God, with his right hand cut off and his left leg!

"Marks—?" I asked, "are you really Marks?"

"You can see," he stammered, "With one limb I testified falsely, the other I cut to soak a stone in the blood. I know that I'm dying now—but I hardly have the right to die—"

I answered him away: "We die if that is God's will!"

He sobbed: "Forgive me, Izidor! May you all forgive me!"

I took pity on him in my heart. "I forgive you, Marks, and I know that Agata has already forgiven you! Because of that you can go before God the judge without worry. May it be forgiven you, so that it may be forgiven us, too!"

"Have the curé come!" he begged.

They called the chaplain, who had a great many duties with burials and last rites, and yet he came quite quickly, because he was not unaware that there was a warrior with an amputated leg who could die at any moment in the ambulatory. They spoke for a long while, during which time the father was writing something down, then he gave the patient absolution and finally guided Marks's left hand for him to make the sign of the holy cross under what the "curé" had written.

And he had written that the heavy cavalryman Marks Wulffing, when he lay wounded in the ambulatory at Turin, humbly and remorsefully acknowledged on his deathbed that at the trial at Loka he had testified falsely against Agata Schwarzkobler, and that everything he had said then was made up and that he asks her and others to forgive and have mercy on him. The "curé" signed this testimony himself and handed it to me.

Later, during the night, Marks Wulffing died. My wish is that the eternal light shine upon him!

When I returned, it was spring: the pear and cherry were in bloom, and the entire Poljane Valley wore a white cloth. Agata and Jurij did not expect me, but they received me as if I had risen from the dead. I was exhausted and the war had rent me. But the two of them embraced me without end and opened their whole house to me. A little girl who could barely crawl was about the house now, and she filled every corner, big and small, with her voice. Now and then a gloom would come over Agata's face and her look would remind me at times of the gaze that on that day, before she stepped into the water, she cast up over the valley.

At that time our pastor was Janez Krstnik Žitnik. The very next day I set off to him and handed him the testimony to which Marks Wulffing had put his cross on his deathbed and the "curé" had signed. Father Janez Krstnik was a just man. Immediately the next Sunday he spoke to the people from the pulpit and explained what wrong was still being done to Agata Khallan, about whom certain people in their Gorenjsko ignorance thought that she probably after all caused hail and storms. He scolded them until many hung their heads, at which point he read Marks's testimony, recounted about his signature, and related how God had struck him in this world when he took his left leg, in which he had cut a wound. The people were moved. Everyone crowded around Agata in front of the church in order to press her hand. That day our lady was honored like a martyr, and the Lord God ordained an end to her suffering. Peter Debelak himself came up to us when we were on the way home from the divine service and he asked to be forgiven. We shook hands and renewed our old friendship.

Contentment came once again to Visoko. The memory of my father Polikarp became blessed, and the blood of the man that had been spilt by his hand no longer called out to God's throne. And the memory of fights and wars left me, except of that one which remained in my breast, where it pecked away at me night and day like a clock hanging on the wall. It weighed upon me, so that I could not take up any sort of work; there was a lot of work, but I was just taking meals at the house! I tried to work but it was impossible, and Jurij and Agata reprimanded me very crudely if I tried to undertake even the most innocent work. It is true that I had not come into the house empty-handed and I could have lived without being a burden upon the household, but a man who cannot work is around the house too much. And that is what was searing me.

When the flowers disappeared from the meadows and gardens and when the heat was coming on, during good weather, I wandered out to the field below the forest, where at one time my father told me that he intended the two Visoko holdings for me. I would lie down in the grass on the exact same spot. Oftentimes I lay so in the sun, the valley sparkling below me; and at such times, that which I had experienced in the past would rise before me. Now and then I was seized by the desire to die because I was a burden on myself and others. But that desire quickly left me because a soldier that lies mortally wounded in the middle of the battlefield is just as unwilling to die as the rich man sitting before a full plate is to part from life.

At such moments I knew well that a strong chain binds you, no matter how abandoned and impoverished you may be, to something of which you are unaware at each instant: that something is—the land on which you were born. That is our one unwavering friend, it always shows you one and the same face and remains faithful to you no matter how many times you disown it! When I lie thus, a new strength rushes from the sod into my weary limbs, and each and every small root beneath me pushes forth into my body, so that I feel at one with the land on which I lie. Native land— not empty words these: it is a part of my life, and if the land is taken from me, life is also taken from me. When you are eaten up to the bones, when you are persecuted everywhere as if mushrooms had sprouted all over your body, your native land will receive you with the same face as it once received you when you were still in a cradle. You have not experienced a spring when you were not embraced by her flowers, and not an autumn when it did not rain fruits upon you. It is possible that it is hard to die—that is not my belief!—but I will also write that I would rather die in the middle of my native valley, be it of hunger, than on the golden throne of the German emperor, where I would have everything in abundance!

Thus I oftentimes ponder things on the green grass below the forest. Now and then I also look into the past: before me stretch out wide ranks of heavily armed men, each rank charges in its turn, the wounded fall and die, rich flags furl, cavalrymen clang on their steeds, generals themselves rush in, "victoria" washes over them, trumpets sound, cannon roar—but all of that disappears as breath disappears from a glass, and only the sweet consciousness remains that I am again on my native land, which embraces me as a mother embraces her child, or as a fiancé her betrothed!

One day I fell asleep beneath the forest and then I awoke again. Helas! How the clock between my lungs began to speed up! Beside me sat Margareta Wulffing, and she did not withdraw her gaze from my face. But wait, she was five years younger than I, consequently she was thirty-seven years old, but she was still a comely woman, for the worries and bitterness she had endured had not yet lined her face.

She spoke up: "Izidor, there was talk that you are weak and that you could really use some tending to."

I did not want to utter a sharp word, yet I unwillingly answered:

"Margareta, haven't you wed yet?" I do not know myself how I arrived at such a query: I was not quite pleased that she had come, because I had not called her.

"Why would I wed?" she sobbed and added: "I could have, after all, there's enough menfolk in the villages who can hardly wait to devour the dowry of a woman who is alone and abandoned."

That I could not deny. Therefore, I simply asked: "What is it you want?"

"But I've already told you," she answered decisively. "I will be a helper to you! You see, after all, that the kin who love you cannot always serve you. There is work in the field, livestock in the barn, and by the time that is done time passes. You do see how Agata presses and the while quakes that you'll be angry if you're not served as should be. —Just don't argue!"

When she talked that way, and when decisiveness welled up in her eyes, she pleased me, a pauper—but it is indeed untoward that I write something like that.

But I did not conquer in that war. Soon Agata also appeared on the field of battle—the two women had surely agreed between themselves—and her army united with Margareta's. They worked me over with musket and cannon for so long that I surrendered to their mercies. I consented, that is, for Margareta Wulffing to come into the house and serve me. And how she served me! She set herself a bed at the door to my small room and if I but coughed a little, wheezed a bit heavily from my pierced lung, in the dark of night she hurried in right away and asked whether I needed this or that.

And one fine day Agata Schwarzkobler again visited. She began to speak seriously about how it could not go on like that, that Margareta was intended for me, that she thought of no one but me, and that for years she was waiting and waiting: and it was not right because of people, and in the parish it had already been noticed that I have an overly young servant woman. I was soon completely surrounded by the enemy and once again I had to surrender! On 29 August 1707, the pastor Father Janez Krstnik wed us in the Poljane church before the altar of the Mother of the Holy Rosary and he spoke beautifully to us. The groom could barely stand, but the bride was nonetheless very happy, and she did not even see how her cousins' chins dropped when I limped out of the church at her side and past the crowd that had come to sate its curiosity. That day the bed of my servant was brought into my room, and Margareta Wulffing became my rightful and true wife!

She served me as before. She cooked every possible sort of thing for me and almost never left me alone. But despite that, she also worked in the house as much as she possibly could. Everyone held her dear, and most of all I, her rightfully wedded husband, loved her. Father Janez Krstnik said many times that she would receive, should she die and should he still be in Poljane then, an inscription on her stone: "Margaretha coelo clemente fruitur," which is supposed to mean: Margareta is most surely deserving of the whole heavenly kingdom!

Postscript

I, Georgius Postumus, son of my father Izidor, born after the death of he who still lives on through my beloved mother Margareta Wulffing, now seventeen years old and in the school of the Ljubljana Jesuit fathers, affirm and testify that our father Izidor ended his years in the Lord on 20 December 1710. He was called away from here and he died easily, and he did not have to bear very great pain at the hour of his death. The day he died he was still going about in the forenoon, but in the afternoon he fell asleep and passed on to the next world as a small yellow autumn leaf that a light breeze blows from the branch. He rests in the cemetery of St. Martin in Poljane, and above him are written the words: "Parva domus—magna quies," which means in our language: A small house—great rest.—May God grant him that rest, and bless Visoko for us, for we are in need of His blessing perhaps no less than Polikarp Khallan, the first master of the two holdings at Visoko!

Heavily indeed God's hand lay upon his children, and it almost seems to us that the blood spilt by Polikarp Khallan is still not satisfied before God's mercy, nor Jošt Schwarzkobler's life, which was sinful.

God's rod beat us. In the year 1716 a merciless murderess wandered home from the Serbian battlefields, a wild plague. At Visoko, it seized and killed the master Jurij and his oldest child, Marija Ana, so that in one week we had two burials.

Both mothers are still living, as well as Suzana, Jurij's daughter, and I, Georgius Postumus, son of Izidor. Consequently, the future of Visoko's two holdings rests on two people. Goody Margareta and Goody Agata quite often put their gray heads together and murmur like two frogs by a well. And now and then my mother in her worldly blindness would quietly and shamelessly hint at this or that.

Even twelve-year old Suzana surprises me sometimes with a look that is almost forbidden between the closest relatives. But everything in me yearns to give my body on the altar and perform the holy service for the souls of those at the Visoko manor who left the world before me and who are yet seeking God's mercy! When after all the most beautiful woman in the world is my good and beloved mother Margareta and when nowhere and nohow do I notice a difference between a young and an old woman—how could I touch another woman, even if that were our tiny Suzana? God only knows how I am to release myself from the distress with which I sigh for him!

Here ends the first Chronicle of Visoko.